Obstacles

Reinhard Lettau

Obstacles

TRANSLATED FROM THE GERMAN BY

Ursule Molinaro

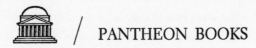

PANTHEON BOOKS

A Division of Random House • NEW YORK

THE TRANSLATOR WISHES TO ACKNOWLEDGE
HER THANKS TO VENABLE HERNDON

Contents

Obstacles

197008

Contents

Enter Manig

Contents

Contents

Obstacles

The Ride

THE NEIGHBORS NOTICED that the three friends who lived in the narrow house, slightly set back from the sidewalk on Mönchstrasse, had lately begun taking their noon outings in a carriage. One day, the dark, completely closed vehicle with unostentatious ornamentation on its doors stood in the semi-circular drive at the foot of the entrance steps, as if it had sprung whole out of the pavement at that very spot. It was an unaccustomed sight, the friends emerging empty-handed from their house, instead of carrying walking sticks. Three abreast they descended to the landing, one tightly beside the other, followed the curve of the steps, stopped at the bottom, approached the carriage three at once. But as the first raises his foot to climb onto the box, the second bars the way with his leg, while the third shakes his head violently. The first retreats a step, two steps, shrugs, seems to give up. Meanwhile the second is preventing the third—with agitated gestures, foot stamping and a variety of grimaces—from climbing onto the box, and the first, getting a fresh start, arrives just in time to pull the wriggling second, who had almost mounted, back into the street. They stand astonished; Indian-file they walk around the back of the carriage, but succeed no better on the other side. The horses stand patiently.

Colonel Wenzel, a neighbor who takes his dessert at this hour by the side window of his alcove that looks out on the friends' house, has a perfect view of the noon spectacle; Colonel Wenzel says that one of the friends sometimes leaps up on the tiny carriage steps, opens the door with lightning speed and tries to persuade his friends with an inviting gesture to climb inside, in the assumption, probably, that he can then nimbly climb onto the box. However, the others usually see through his ruse before that moment, and the friend makes his inviting gesture to empty air. Nobody climbs in, says Wenzel, and since the other two never leave without the third, nor wish to let him take up his humble seat on the box, the ride cannot take place; all three go back in for their walking sticks and set out on foot as always and ever.

Their ruses are manifold. A cream puff in his left hand, a cigarette in his right, Wenzel has observed many a curious spectacle. It may, for instance, happen that the three friends walk up to the carriage with seemingly casual, inattentive steps, but then rapidly walk away from it again with exag-

gerated gestures, tiptoe around it, invite each other with
measured bows to jump onto the box or the small steps. Or
they may bend double, almost touching the pavement, trying
to discover the others' plans in time. At this point all three
may stand on their heads or lie under the carriage in brotherly unison, get up, dust off their clothes. Or they may
emerge from the house and immediately take up positions at
considerable distance from the carriage itself, in the courtyard, in the street, under the porte-cochere of a neighboring
house: strategic posts which, although unsuited for rapid attack on the carriage and the coveted box, as experience has
taught them, will however nail the others firmly in their
places. Many a cream puff has been squashed between the
colonel's excited fingers when they nevertheless in one bound
leaped to the unguarded positions. For the duration of a
second all three could be seen standing together on the roof
of the swaying vehicle, staring at each other with embarrassed faces. At other times all three found themselves sitting
astride the lead horse; uncounted are the leaps that were
executed, the positions that were taken.

If modesty and all-around consideration for equality
among the friends had been offered as the explanation of
these noontime incidents that seemed to center on the driver's box to which no one wanted to see the others, and to
which each wanted to see himself degraded—i.e. if the
friends' mutual awareness of their equality toward each other
had been advanced as the justification—it was all the more
disconcerting to observe the opposite spectacle a few weeks

later, when the quarrel seemed to be about the seats in the comfortable interior of the luxurious vehicle. Again the friends would step out of their house, but now noticeably elegant, dressed like country squires, again it would come to apparently undesirable sneak tactics like pacing up and down, again they would alternately invite each other to sit on the box, to climb inside, again there would be sudden leaps, and the three gentlemen would find themselves one on top of the other in the hemp-colored interior, while the doors continued to dangle outward for a long time afterwards. The good soldier Wenzel read consternation on the friends' faces, just as he was about to reach for a delicate creamed edifice. As though anesthetized they remained sitting in the vibrating structure, as though they expected some helpful power to bring the horses to a slow trot, and grace all three of them with the longed-for cradle-soothing pleasure of a ride together.

It never came to that. Yet, the friends must have gained a clear insight into their situation from this last experience, because the next day all three could be seen stepping out of the house in finely tailored lackeys' liveries. With firm, unmistakable gait they approached the much-disputed vehicle, and while one mounted the box one could see the other two climb up on the footmen's crosswise jump-board in back. Two pairs of hands clutched the shiny brass grips, two heads rested for an instant, it seemed, on the carriage roof, two stiff forms peered over it, obsequiously ready to jump down at any moment. The driver turned his head to the back and the enfuriated Wenzel noticed that all three were smiling at one another as the whip snapped the signal for departure. People in the street who watched the elegant vehicle roll by were never able to look into the interior of the carriage. Thick silk curtains screened it from the eyes of the crowd.

The Maze

THE EAST WING had been completed and the gardens
that had been laid out on the somewhat extended property
were just now in bloom, Edward, Provincial Governor in
Muggensturm, wrote to his beloved wife who was spending a
few months in the south. The scarcities and difficulties of the
first post-war years had been overcome—the house of which
they had been deprived for so long was again liveable to its
last nook and cranny, interior and exterior damage had been
repaired, and an adequate number of newly liveried servants
was once more at their disposal. This favorable change of
conditions—not a change, actually, as Dorothea well knew, a
reinstatement rather of former, well-deserved, in a way
merely interrupted privileges—this restoration of long-ac-
quired wealth to which he, Edward, had been entitled since

birth, was more apparent now than it had been in February, when his beloved wife, weary of the native climate and following the doctors' suggestions, had departed for sunnier horizons. And now the gardens had been entrusted to the expert care of Mr. Wolterbeek, a Dutchman. The letter closed with a few heart-felt expressions of Edward's desire for his wife's prompt return, though only from a distance, since he did not wish to press her too forcibly; and without mention of the maze which the governor was having built as a surprise for Dorothea.

Edward's entourage had agreed from the start not to reveal his little secret before his wife's return, since the governor hoped to fulfill a mutually nurtured long-term desire with the construction of the maze. The laying out of the rest of the garden favored their vow of secrecy—relatives who came to visit and intimate friends were left in the dark as to the significance of the extensive construction. Even before presentation of the first blueprints Wolterbeek remarked that a maze was the most brotherly combination of art and nature. Baroque in form, but extremely natural in its essence—by its very imitation of nature's aimlessness, of its chaotic entanglement—it reinstated nature in its original, dignified position.

All the same, the Dutchman had permitted himself certain deviations from the strictly baroque style which concerned not so much the maze itself but its relationship to the surrounding landscape. The architect did not wish to see the maze a thing apart, bordered by the rest of a noncommittal landscape "as though it were a playground for people to go in and out of," he wanted it reasonably integrated into the existing landscape, in direct proximity—especially the entrance and the exit—to the stairs that swept up to the main house. The plans suggested that the entrance to the maze be placed just inside the wide gates that led into all of the governor's lands, namely on the road to the main house. And so a stretch of the wide asphalt road was incorporated in the labyrinth since, according to Wolterbeek's plans, its exact entrance could not be accurately defined. It was hardly discernible, even when consulting the plans, before the construction was finished and gave rise to countless conversations. While Edward, incidentally somewhat annoyed by the constant changes among the workmen who had been hired for the planting of the park—new workmen had to be hired constantly, but never seemed to stay very long; one day they would simply fail to report to work and were often missed by their families, had joined the foreign legion, apparently—while Edward was under the impression that the maze proper began at the spot at which the paving of the thus-far comfortable driveway stopped and gradually, irregularly narrowed, and at which the surrounding hedges began to grow higher and evener, Wolterbeek curiously moved the entrance of the maze directly to the gates of the governor's estates; in the course of several conversations, the builder, whom Edward's doubtful glances could scarcely restrain, even wanted to start the maze far beyond his client's estates and pick up broad stretches of Baden and Alemania to connect into the antechambers of the labyrinth.

That it began, or at least might begin, at the spot that

Wolterbeek had indicated, proved to be true one morning when the long-announced official visit of the governor of the neighboring province, an extremely dependable man named Teitge, which had been definitely set for that specific day, failed to take place. Edward had abandoned the administrative buildings of his predecessor, which were located in Muggensturm proper, to the grateful county and discharged his official duties from his own home; that morning about seven o'clock, as he was sitting early at his desk, he thought he heard the sound of automobiles approaching. He prepared to jump up and hurry out to meet the expected visitor, when the vehicles seemed to be driving off again. Even the mail from Dorothea which he received the following morning, announcing her return for the same day, could not relieve the irritation Edward felt because the visit of his governmental colleague, much desired if only for political reasons, had failed to materialize.

To put himself in the mood for his beloved wife's consoling return, he went for a stroll, which led him deep into the maze that had been built chiefly in her honor. The silence of the now wide, now narrow paths that kept opening into squares in which the stroller paused to turn several times, but had to abandon because they led nowhere—the seclusion of this cool, formal landscape soon put him in a happy mood. After a lengthy walk he had, at one point, the surprise to find his house practically on top of him, on the other side of an impenetrable hedge. But he turned pale when, at the edge of a wider path, he ran into Teitge whose gasoline had given out after an endless drive far into the night and who was continuing his journey on foot in the company of his escort. The hungry man manifested amusement when he heard how close he had been to his destination for twenty-four hours. He assured Edward that he found the joke delightful, but that the final rescue was particularly praiseworthy. Laughing they set out; Edward's sure eye eliminated wrong turns which he did not even deem worthy of a few hesitant steps. Stepping briskly, they suddenly ran into a hedge that blocked their path; they were forced to turn back; still joking Teitge threatened, and raised his index finger. "To the kitchen," he cried, "lead us to the kitchen!" His colleague's bantering tone disappeared when Edward, still stepping briskly, repeatedly led them up to high hedge walls, which caused delays, because the gentlemen in the rear of Teitge's escort would have to be asked to step backward to get out of the blind alley for Edward to remain their guide at the head of the group. Most of the time these retreats had something ballet-like about them—the gentlemen would hold on to each others' hips—which prompted giggling or loud laughter among the gayer participants; under peals of laughter the line would wind its polonaise way now out of one, now out of another wrong path. These retreats turned out to be most wise; Edward was still at the head of the troupe when, behind the sharp curve of a path, that turned out to be a blind alley, he ran smack into the remains of several workmen who must have been left behind at this spot during the construction. There was no time to conceal the sight from Teitge who was walking immediately behind his host—while they hastily backed out, which prompted immediate laughter in the rear, he pensively bowed his head. On a green carpet they later also found the body of Otto, Edward's favorite butler who had run away weeks ago across the border, as Edward had concluded at the time.

The gentlemen in Teitge's escort choked on their giggles. They had pressed too close too fast, invited by the square-like widening of the trick path. After short consultation the troupe re-formed in the usual fashion, but did not move from the spot, because laughter rose from another side. The source of this new gaiety was Wolterbeek, who could now be seen standing next to the fragile figure of a woman on the balcony of the governor's house in the distance, a sight which had escaped the gentlemen because of their meeting with Otto.

"I've given instructions," the Dutchman called over— while Dorothea, whom Edward was now able to make out as the female figure by his side, turned tenderly toward him— "for considerable expansion of the maze; in right-angled versatility it will extend far beyond my estates. While your group supposes the exit behind each leaf-shaded dead end, the maze actually continues in all directions into a planned landscape which reinstates nature, after a detour of discipline, in all its autonomy, its beautiful dignity. But even there—even if your guests were to sight a village or a tavern behind the turn of a path—even there they have not escaped the labyrinth."

The gentlemen who heard this stood in stunned silence. But colleague Teitge cried, "Onward, onward. Let us find that tavern," and they danced off, with Edward at the end of the troupe.

A New Timetable

FREQUENTLY, when an express train carried Mr. Muck-Bruggenau springily across the countryside, he'd think that his name might easily be given to almost any of the smaller towns through which the express was just then disdainfully racing, and that no one would know the difference. "Straight out of the timetable," he'd murmur to himself, while his knowing eye checked the signals and track markers that were flying past outside.

To the consternation of friends who might be travelling with him, his sensitive ear could, from great distances, discern differences between the tatatatatata of a local and the tatáta tatáta tatáta of an express; eyes closed he could tell if they were entering a large station or a small station, or if they were going to stop, all by the rhythm of the wheels flying across a switch. While the other passengers, horribly bored, stared sleepily out the window until the telegraph wires that were slithering past, now up, now down, made them dizzy, Muck-Bruggenau sat, an unabridged edition of the Railroad Timetable in his lap, checking connecting trains or, during the conductor's visit, shooting out expert answers before the man was able to supply a curious traveller with information. The very sight of the Unabridged Timetable stirred his senses and every six months he'd greet the new edition the way a poet greets spring. Before starting his thorough study he'd pat it from all sides, roll it up, hide it in the hollow of his hand and then let it purr open over his thumb. He'd listen to the dull slapping sound it made when dropped to the floor and enjoy the pale green and pink of the pages, whose color code he had of course long ago deciphered.

On free afternoons or after office hours—he practiced law—he rushed to the central station. He was stirred to passion by the clunk of the machine dispensing his platform ticket, by the platform guard's punching a hole in it; then the way to the tracks was clear; he knew exactly where to go, when not to miss important trains. He'd see a giant locomotive approach and pass, for instance, on Track 2A, watch it come to a smoking stop in front of nonchalantly waiting people with suitcases and soon make sure, with knowing eye, which cars stood where, how old they were, what numbers they bore; in a flash he'd gain a picture of the train's quality.

He had no eye for the people who streamed out of the long-distance expresses or commuter trains, unless they were railroad employees whose rank he could tell by a rapid, singularly envious glance at their epaulettes. If all was in good order, and after he had listened to the always much too brief, but at least accurate announcements of the loudspeaker, he'd walk up to the information man whose yellow visor he had not let out of sight. In the beginning, the curt, distant manner in which these men discharged their duties almost turned his stomach. But when he realized what petty, insignificant questions were being asked here day in day out, especially by brazen-faced travellers of low station, he began to sympathize with the disappointment, not to say the indignation, of the information officials, who never seemed allowed to plumb the true depths of the timetable, to propose audacious changes or to unmask nonexisting connections, in a word: to satisfy and answer an authentic search. Too rarely a gentleman of the world would step up—empty-handed, as though strolling down the promenade, his luggage already on its way to his hotel, distributed among a pack of porters—and ask demanding, practically unanswerable questions that excited the imagination, about which one could go on thinking in one's bed, hearing the 0:21 whistle in the distance, noting that its entry was blocked, as usual.

He often thought about how few travellers were really searching. He would sit at home, shaking his head, reading the timetable, comparing train numbers, adding track mileage, circling junctions with a red pencil. He began to suspect that the present timetable (and all its previous editions), although quite clear and rationally composed, completely omitted a higher intangible that lay within the schedules themselves. The importance of the destination of a traveller questioning the book was especially overrated. This particular circumstance made for the superficial thoroughness of the book. Therefore he decided to work out a new timetable for the whole country. At first he based his work on fictitious distances and places, including his own name, which fulfilled a secret dream, and then began all over again between Nurnberg and Fürth, and only gradually worked his way up to the North-South Express and related subjects. Although he fitted himself completely into the existing network, he nevertheless suffered many reversals. For instance he discovered one morning that, because of a simple mathematical miscalculation, two long-distance express trains had been racing into one another nightly for two weeks between Tiefenbrunn and Meuth-Landhaus. Or, after careful study of his schedule, Muck-Bruggenau would discover derailments, or an international express that lay blocked at the southern border, or even trains—he thought of D-390—that had tracelessly vanished between two towns, because they simply had no assigned destination. Such discoveries would make him suffer.

During long sleepless nights such errors were spotted and corrected. The practical experience he acquired—also during night hours when there was no one to surprise him—was of valuable assistance. He had no trouble purchasing the traditional headgear of an information official and when a train pulled in, he'd quickly put the cap on his head, although he never went as far as stepping out of the dark corner where he knew he was safe. At first only isolated travellers would come to him—travellers who'd take the trouble to look for him, who'd hurry up to him once they had spotted him and ask for desperately needed information—but this soon changed; he'd inform them so well, with accuracy as well as wit, that his reputation seemed to spread by word of mouth. Once a genuine, rightfully appointed information official walked up to him; Muck-Bruggenau noticed him too late to save himself by rapid removal of his cap. But his fears were unfounded, as he could tell by the adoring, euphoric look in the expert's eye. The man stood motionless, like a signal post, an abandoned track light, intoxicated with Muck-Bruggenau's knowledge, and after Muck-Bruggenau's information period was over, the station master, who had also joined the listening group, raised his signal lamp high above his head in humble homage.

After this experience, Muck-Bruggenau's conduct grew bolder. Perhaps the other railroad employees had tacitly decided not to say anything because of the stranger's unusual gifts, perhaps they tolerated him because he did, after all, relieve them of a part of their job—now they did not have to stand around the tracks on biting winter nights, but could sit in the well-heated booth and drink tea with rum—or perhaps because they thought that they were face to face with a secret envoy from the central administration—at any rate, no one objected. This lack of opposition kindled in Muck-Bruggenau the irresistible temptation to base his information not on the generally accepted schedule, but on his own work which had by now been completed. The numerous members of a children's camp were the first to fall victims to this experiment. Luckily they were eager to travel, because an extremely long trip was lying ahead of them. Under the guidance of credulous counselors who had taken Muck-Bruggenau's connections to heart, they rode about the countryside for weeks before they arrived at their destination, exhausted but happy. A similar fate befell a company of infantrymen whose leader memorized Muck-Bruggenau's information and set out on an expedition with his men. Generally speaking Muck-Bruggenau was particularly successful with tours. Only one person, the group leader, had to be won over and immediately Muck-Bruggenau had a numerous following.

Actually the new timetable was not vastly different from the standard work. The two editions agreed almost completely on times of departure. But there was contradiction as to the promised places of destination. As long as the followers of the Muck-Bruggenau schedule were in the minority, they had to change trains frequently, according to tables Muck-Bruggenau would show them. But once they were in the majority—increasing demand had prompted the author to circulate his timetable among information officials throughout the country—it could come to their simply forcing the conductor to stop his train in an open field, by pulling the emergency cord, and holding certain, never-till-then-seen figures under the helpless man's nose before asking him to remember the number of his own train and to back up and follow the route as directed by the new timetable. Eventually trains announced in the regular railroad timetable were running only on paper. But on the basis of the new work one could confidently plan a trip even to remote areas which the new timetable had not yet reached; the trip merely took longer, led to detours and frequent train changes, but permitted people who would never have risked such adventures on their own to see ravishing parts of the country, and sent them, perhaps for the first time in their lives, in search of a destination: a search that was actually more desirable than the destination itself and that often made them forget it. The services of the information officials whom Muck-Bruggenau personally instructed became invaluable. They supplied the public with well-reasoned oracles that were carefully adapted to the special case of each individual searcher; it was an entirely new type of service and one could foresee that they would eventually form an entirely new caste.

It is not surprising that comments began to appear in all parts of the country. Fabulous combinations were suggested and willingly tried out. Praise is due the man who pointed out that the intangible, the need for which Muck-Bruggenau hailed in florid language, did indeed exist in his work: the fictitious town of Muck-Bruggenau, which the author must have forgotten to remove during the transition from his first draft to the definitive edition of the timetable—this place, for which there was, of course, no geographic proof, might even be considered the focal point of the entire network.

It had to be imagined somewhere inside the busy traffic triangle between Talbrugg–Schollerach–Talen-Eggeln. According to the schedule, trains were constantly arriving at that spot, thirsty locomotives were served with water, hundreds of tons of freight were handled. The vertical lines on a schedule which indicate the racing through of long-distance trains all came to an abrupt stop at Muck-Bruggenau; it was a traffic center of the first magnitude. An irrational quantity had without a doubt crept into Muck-Bruggenau's calculations, but it did not annul his calculations in any way; on the contrary, it fulfilled them beautifully. According to his schedule, almost all trains touched this place at one time or another during their trip—perhaps at a moment when all passengers were asleep, so that they never saw the red-capped master of this particular station raise the signal for departure as he watched the never-ending flow of trains.

Muck-Bruggenau successfully resisted suggestions to build this place and make it real. But he settled in the spot where one might assume its existence, if it did exist; and now he could feel—whether sitting in an armchair or busy with the roses outside in his garden—that he was constantly in the center of a railroad network whose tracks spanned the country in a new way.

Punishing the Guest

FOR SEVERAL WEEKS the guest had kept them waiting in vain for his arrival. The spacious house was ready to receive him, the bed in the sumptuous guest suite had been made up with the finest linen, flowers had been put in vases, the kitchen was filled with an aroma of salads mixed by expert hands, but the guest wasn't arriving. The first hours of unfulfilled expectation were the most painful—at what point could they be sure that the guest was no longer arriving? He was coming from afar and had announced his arrival for an indefinite hour that afternoon.

Since then, well-composed cables had postponed his arrival from day to day. His explanations grew more substantial, the words were more and more carefully chosen, and when a superbly phrased excuse arrived on the morning of the third day, they had to admit secretly that these cables made the guest's delays almost fascinating. Each time a new arrival drew near, they surprised themselves thinking that a new wire would be preferable to the mere arrival of the guest himself, because the reasons for his delays were so varied and unexpected that all soon began to say that the guest's actual arrival would have come as an anticlimax.

Obviously the daily recurrence of fruitless waiting, that would drop to zero only to rise again telegraphically, disturbed the order of the household. It was especially painful when a new cable delayed the arrival for a couple of hours or half a day, and all preparations had to be halted, or at least interrupted. The hosts had to resort to hasty interim arrangements and often a new wire resetting the guest's announced arrival would throw them into utmost excitement. At that point, the salads, that the previous cable had threatened with wilting, had been devoured, the silver trays had been stacked away, the house wasn't ready any more. It's not surprising that, after a week, the possibility of the guest's failing to arrive was included in the preparations for his arrival. The periodical preparation for the guest's possible non-arrival required a different set-up. Much had to be taken into consideration and planned for, but there was one other alternative: to keep the house in a state of permanent readiness. But in order to achieve this, the hosts would have had to leave their house, keeping it untouched by the changing course of events, and watch the guest's actual arrival, perhaps from a neighboring house—their ready house in constant view.

Punishing the Guest

The hosts' mood turned sour when they realized that the guest had kept them waiting for two weeks. At first, the constant announcements of his arrival for the next day or the next hour might have given an impression of optimism; but by now there was little doubt that the classical period of his cable-literature was apparently over. On the seventeenth day, toward noon, they received a cable: "Arriving immediately," and spontaneously invited by telephone all the friends and neighbors who had been supposed to be present at the reception of the guest from the start. Together with the neighbors and friends a telegraph boy arrived at the house, delivering a threadbare epic by the once-again-not-arriving visitor.

The friends entered the house, chatting loudly in expectation of the guest. This splendid summer day was certainly deserving of praise, they remarked, and walked straight through the house into the garden. Here they stood together on tender strips of lawn, lauding their host's horticultural talents. Nothing, they cried, could spoil their mood, nor did they manifest any disappointment when their host proceeded to read them the just-received cable—on the contrary: they immediately wanted all the preceding messages read to them as well. This was done, and great hilarity broke out when they discovered that the twelfth telegram from the vainly awaited guest had been sent from a town nearby, that the guest must therefore have passed through the area, whereas his most recent messages had come from Hammerfest.

The idea to play at arrival-of-the-guest came from Mrs. Saatmantel, a voluminous widow. It was applauded by all and Theodore, the oldest son of the house, jumped from a kitchen window, tiptoed around the driver's box and mounted a rented vehicle that transported him in no time in front of the parental house. A servant opened the carriage door for him; waving a weary left hand toward the house, he handed the servant an impressive tip. On the terrace he was embraced and introduced all around. He gave lengthy accounts of the unpleasantness of his delays, drank a number of highballs, and in the general gaiety no one paid particular attention to the fact that the real guest, a Mr. Flugbeil, had actually arrived in the meantime and was standing among the servants. When Flugbeil had reached the house shortly after Theodore, well-informed friends had dragged him into the cellar and clad him in butler's livery. To this day he is serving with zeal, although he's been known to turn pale occasionally when there is talk of a guest arriving.

A Campaign

HESITATION, pondering a matter before arriving at a decision, seemed the highest of military gifts to General von Unkugen. He did not like to see young men on his staff showing their recklessness by having prompt suggestions at all times at the tips of their tongues, nor was he fond of gentlemen who, after long reflection, came up with notions that were, in themselves, not worthy of even a moment's thought; in a word: he favored intelligent reflection, moderately quick, fruitful thinking. During meetings he could be seen bent over the map, which he always knew to the last detail, every hill, mound, canal, lake, house and field—he could be seen bending over the map, his hand darting here and there, closing over a village, pointing to a wooded area, falling into a crossroad, approaching valleys with extended

A Campaign

index finger, almost dying, with upturned palm, in remoter regions.

"Who besides myself knows how to make a decision?" he cried. "How to think a matter through from all angles, how to keep both eyes open to all eventualities, how to be constantly prepared so that even failure, the very worst, is still welcome—all this means that, sometimes, we must not act at all, that we must sit quietly by the fireside, with our hands in our laps, and stare into the flames while something happens somewhere else."

The gentlemen of the staff who had been called in to discuss the situation at the front on the morning of November fourth, listened to von Unkugen's words and said nothing. For weeks their chief had permitted no changes in the deployment of the front lines, not even in those places where contact with the enemy had taken place. But the enemy, under Marshal Kalcavsky, didn't seem eager for a meeting either. At any rate, he hadn't gone beyond skirmishes which secured existing positions without provoking changes—local advances that seemed to say, "I'm still around!" But no more. Captain Dottelein, a talented young man, opened the meeting by reading the daily account of the situation; only its date made it different from the daily accounts of the past months, although the choice of words and the syntax had been improved and there were a few daring stylistic innovations—Dottelein was a stylist; he never stopped polishing—which surprised the gentlemen. They learned that there had been no changes in the situation. Local patrols had irritated

Kalcavsky here and there, had approached a wooded area in the north, but had quickly withdrawn at the first signs of resistance. Nödelchen had also annoyed the enemy, but yielded any territorial gains the minute the other side disputed them. The day's report closed with rows of internal figures, statistics and administrative modifications. Von Unkugen did not listen to the end. He thanked Dottelein and turned his attention to the maps, where Colonel de Guilloton, a doctor of mathematics and lover of geography, stood ready to deliver his lecture.

"When," he began, having been handed the familiar yellow pointer, "when," because he was fond of asking questions, "when is a decision made? At this point, or that? Should one permit an approaching event to occur, should one whisper into the ear of one's adjutant and order him to present said event to the world as completed action, as a fact? Or should one wait a moment longer?"

"Where," the gentlemen drew closer, "is a decision made?" If one wishes to force a decision at whatever spot one happens to be standing, one deprives oneself of one's moving potential, which quite obviously requires space: one fights sitting down. But if, just for the sake of hypothesis, one were to imagine a tidy landscape void of all geographical sloppiness—the pointer advanced to a position shamefully distant from the actual front lines, approximately two hundred day-marches away—if then one imagined an area almost totally free of hills, unexpected depressions or other equally distorting elements, no one would, even under such absolute, landscape-less conditions, think of forcing a decision at this spot or that. To evoke such clean, neat conditions was a luxury, but it did refresh the mind and clear the way for new thoughts.

De Guilloton was followed by Ziervogel, one of Nödel-chen's men, who was later followed by Hatius, representative of the right flank, who discussed the further reinforcement of the present positions, a plan he both approved and recommended. By the time von Unkugen dismissed the gentlemen of the staff, one had gotten the general impression that the decision to stage a battle was not likely to be made at present.

The next morning during second breakfast, which von Unkugen was taking in the company of de Guilloton and Dottelein and which was completely dominated by de Guilloton's utterances about a certain Hume, David—as usual Dottelein kept a notebook open on his left knee so he could jot down any ideas his chief or de Guilloton might have; under the table, without disturbing the casual atmosphere of the meal—during second breakfast an artillery attack was launched against Hatius's flank. De Guilloton, who had stopped speaking after the first reports arrived, watched von Unkugen flush with rage, push his chair back from the table and rise to his feet. "What is the meaning of this?" he shouted and demanded reports. They arrived, revealing minor losses. "It is clear," cried von Unkugen, "Kalcavsky is trying to create the impression that he is weak on Nödel-chen's side, but strong on the left. We shall meet him!"

A Campaign

And when Hatius's flank launched an attack against Kalcavsky's left that very same day, while Nödelchen's troops were gradually pulled over to Hatius's side to reinforce the attacking wedge, it became clear that the enemy had, indeed, feigned strength on the left. Hatius's men took almost empty positions, held only by skeleton forces that either hastily abandoned them or willingly surrendered. Kalcavsky's men retreated so nimbly that it was difficult to maintain contact and to determine the direction of the advance. After several days the advance came to a halt, finally meeting with emphatic resistance along the entire front, and it became apparent that Kalcavsky's right flank, led by Carsch, had advanced in turn and occupied Nödelchen's almost empty positions, since his forces had been pulled out to reinforce Hatius's attack. The two sides had described a circle around each other, and were now facing each other from opposite fronts, without damage to either. It all went to show, as de Guilloton concluded in a lecture he was called upon to deliver, that if one built one's plan on a ruse, one had to be prepared to have one's ruse detected. When both sides resorted to this tactic, the enemies cancelled each other's advances, as mathematical principle would indicate, and the battle became a feat of the imagination.

This became more and more evident in the course of the weeks that followed. When von Unkugen, cautious as usual, attacked a certain sector, Kalcavsky would meet the attack with precision and rapidity. When von Unkugen moved his troops in a threatening fashion, a countermeasure on the other side of the line would promptly not only give the initiative back to Kalcavsky, who would have in turn revealed his own threatening ideas, but would also lock both sides in the old equilibrium, should Unkugen decide to attack in earnest.

The capitals of the combatant countries were not pleased with this development. Reports named empty areas that had been occupied, told of resisting the enemy at unimportant spots, not even in the proximity of oases. Much to the regret of the respective governments, the front lines expanded, completely indifferent to the condition of either enemy's native soil, but the soldiers were in good shape. If enemy troops appeared unexpectedly outside the gates of the capital of one warring country, this did not mean that the war had been lost, since no one was certain that one's own army was not at the same moment relaxing in the enemy capital. Because troops were constantly on the march toward new strategic points, and conditions changed so rapidly at times, Kalcavsky's units could be seen voluntarily marching beside one's own men on their way to somewhere. That, as a matter of fact, is how Nödelchen's much disliked adjutant was lost to Unkugen's staff. Dottelein claimed, not without a trace of irony—his notebook had reaped a rich harvest after the incident—that his camp was happy to renounce such a bothersome bellyacher.

Soon after that the armies executed several outright circular movements. At one point, after both sides had once again been unable to avoid them, Kalcavsky and Unkugen found themselves face to face in the latter's headquarters. Unkugen immediately turned to leave, but overheard Kalcavsky, who had a reputation for wit, telling de Guilloton that he needn't bother rolling up the maps as he was about to do, and that he could leave the pointer as well, and in all good faith, since the same had been done at Kalcavsky's headquarters which was at their disposal on the other side of the front. This offer started a new phase; both armies began leaving all kinds of equipment behind in their respective positions; often the men would flit, at times even bareheaded, in and out of enemy positions, now retrieving an enemy tool, now one of their own, more familiar, undamaged and all in one piece. Now with yellow pointer, now with a lovely green one—which he had found in Kalcavsky's headquarters—de Guilloton directed the eyes of the staff (that became more and more varied; one day they were even able to welcome Kalcavsky's adjutant, the Baron d'O) far beyond the present trenches toward tidy, flat, ideal spaces.

The absolute campaign—d'O notwithstanding—could never progress beyond initial, uninvolving skirmishes, since both sides were obliged to think twice about starting operations that included in their plan every possible enemy countermeasure. Was one not obliged to suspect therefore that, after so many inconsequential contacts, a final victory would, in spite of logical thinking, only bring embarrassment to both sides? Who was to say whether the potential conqueror would not renounce all tangible demonstration of his victory?

A *Campaign*

Although there could be no certainty as to the outcome, there was fear in some quarters that any too sudden change in the front lines might put both commanders once again, by now wiser, on the same side; and as no one could equal the combined knowledge of the two, it was expected that the fortunate army, thus unexpectedly endowed with two heads, would necessarily win. In order to forestall this danger, an exchange of commanders rather than of positions was soon begun, since one could only reluctantly admit that all operations had, up to now, resulted in nothing but an exchange of positions.

The gentlemen were kept under constant observation when they emerged from their trenches at a specified hour and walked toward the enemy positions; a number of rules were set up, preventing any unauthorized communication between the two halfway between lines—each knew the other's language and insisted that all tactical problems be outlined in both languages, so deeply did each believe in the fact-forming power of the original—and forbidding them to march together toward any one side. These rules transformed the exchange of commanders into a ceremony which, like all ceremonies, soon drowned its initial purpose in a flood of color and pomp. Years later, even older recruits had trouble remembering what that purpose had been. They often looked embarrassed when newcomers asked why the two aging commanders walked—at least once a week, or occasionally, when the applause kept on and cries of bis and encore would not stop, several times in the course of the same after-

A Campaign

noon—with measured steps and to the sound of stately marches toward the enemy lines and disappeared behind them. Several years later, younger officers, who had only recently been pronounced fit for battle, and arrived fresh from home, eager to return there, submitted a proposal to simplify the ceremony. It was enthusiastically accepted. After several decades, when everyone had grown tired of carrying the, by now, ancient warriors, who were no longer able to walk, pantingly across no man's land—a task entrusted to a lieutenant and three sergeants—the fighting troops, to the joy of the population, returned to their respective capitals, while the two grizzled commanders, von Unkugen and Kalcavsky, every so often exchanged orders in writing until, at the proper time, a third man assumed this duty, but for both simultaneously, as well as for de Guilloton, Dottelein and d'O, and for all time to come.

Invitation to Summer Thunderstorms

EVERY SUMMER the widow Saatmantel, whose youth belongs to legend, sends out invitations to thunderstorms. When the sun broods day after day outside the tightly shuttered windows, uninterrupted by a hasty shower or even a steady downpour, an invitation is bound to arrive at any moment. Messengers bring the small envelopes to one's house and no butler's thumb will hesitate to retrace the well-phrased text: it is embossed. One learns that, heaven permitting, one has been invited to a thunderstorm for the same evening; one sets out at once.

The small road through Rastatt is always stimulating for the first few miles. Perhaps because of the nearness of the mountains or the narrowness of this still flat, though winding, stretch of road, the landscape seems to shrink, contracting at left and at right to a steadily diminishing, more readily overseeable smallness and withdrawing almost completely: the world becomes a path that leads directly, thirstily, to the country seat of the widow Saatmantel.

After one leaves the narrow road, one drives through a single gate; the carriage slumps into a slow, dark trot, one can hear the fine gravel under the gnashing wheels. Behind the house one finds the vehicles of the other guests parked in the coincidental array of their arrival—their hesitation as to which spot to choose still visible by the odd angles of their wheels. The tables have been set in front of the house; one is almost surprised to find them so overloaded in view of the anticipated natural event. The elegant dresses of the ladies— wide, fluffy gowns with a variety of the most expensive cor- sages, the dark suits of the men, with white handkerchiefs puffing from the breast pockets like escaping sails, the casu- ally held glasses, and finally the seductive music that melts strangely into the trees, make one forget the approaching storm.

Still, once the meal is under way, the anticipated thunder- storm never fails to be mentioned. Every time, as long as anyone can remember, Henri Plein, a higher secretary of justice, has stood up and expressed the hope that, on this particular occasion, there would be a French thunderstorm. He insists that the proximity of the border permits such wishful dreams, and says he feels sorry for anyone unfamiliar with the French storms, which are infinitely wittier than the German ones. Such speeches provoke contradiction, of

course; still, no one knows quite why Mrs. Blesse, an otherwise critical expert, insists on directing the attention of the
outraged guests to Ganghofer thunderstorms. No matter
what speculations are made as to the quality of the anticipated thunderstorm, one can always tell that Mrs. Saatmantel does not enjoy hearing them. The widow seems, on
the contrary, bent on making her guests forget the approach
of the storm, even when deep growling and the first heavy
drops plainly announce its imminent arrival. And yet the
widow knows that it will never again happen as spontaneously as it did several years ago, during a summer garden
party that had been planned as that and nothing else, when a
thunderstorm chased an excited, partly screaming crowd into
the narrow foyer of her house—and obliged a Mr. Wurf, a
charmer with intoxicating features, to stay the night because
his clothes were completely soaked. It was then that the idea
of planning future summer parties so as to have them
crowned by a storm suggested itself—an expensive idea, incidentally, because many pieces of furniture are ruined each
time by the violent downpours, as one can observe from the
windows.

For the first few years it was difficult to find orchestras to
play at these thunderstorm parties, since it had become
known in musicians' circles that these engagements, though
generously remunerated, were most troublesome and essen-
tially degrading—since the gentlemen would often be urged
to continue playing in the pouring rain: damaged instruments, warped violins for instance, were the result. The mu-

sicians felt that this was undignified, since one could not hear the music through the tightly shut windows of the sheltering house, and the amused guests could see the gentlemen playing their instruments only for fractions of seconds during flashes of lightning. They'd stand huddled together, bluish-green and wide-eyed, a brass tuba or violin bow raised motionless toward the sky, a cluster resembling a single icicle, or as though posed for a photographer. Behind the streaming windows they'd see the faces of the guests, distorted with shouts of laughter. The widow earned great praise for this effect, which proved her sense of the dramatic, but still it had to be given up because lightning kept striking the flawless silver of the trumpets. Today therefore, as soon as the rain starts, the gentlemen begin to play on fake instruments which they have brought along for this purpose. Once these instruments have grown soft with rain, the gentlemen are asked into the house, where a hearty bouillon awaits them.

There is no lack of chaos inside the house, once the party has managed to save itself. Dripping dresses are wrung out, large puddles form in the salons on the ground floor and it must be mentioned that, during a flash of lightning or when a loud thunder clap makes the windows rattle, there are dozens of frightened embraces. While night is visibly falling outside and a pale reflection of distant lightning holds the company in suspense, more than one butler has felt the widow's heavy hand on his arm, even with great emphasis, and no one can say how many guests are forced to spend the night. Enough dry clothes are not always available and one has to resort to outlandish costumes: masks appear, a kind of improvised carnival. Behind hurriedly put-up screens one hears laughter. A rustling fire in the fireplace casts shadows across the room; a feeling of sudden isolation from the outside world spreads a strange mood. It is hard to suppress the suspicion that the widow Saatmantel, a gay though somewhat curious lady, sends out invitations to summer thunderstorms precisely because she knows in what intimacies and sensations an event of nature always unites a group of people, and because she foresees such a general world-loving mood.

Potemkin's Carriage
Passes Through

April 11, 1784

LAST NIGHT we received orders from Sebastopol to remain here and await further instructions. It seems that we are to be kept here even after the carriage has passed through. It makes sense; we have travelled a great distance from our native villages, and even before we began building this village we had to prepare regular sleeping accommodations for ourselves. We began by building simple huts, for which we used part of the government material slated for the construction of the make-believe village. Then we built the housefronts of the village they had ordered onto our modest lodgings on either side of the road. My quarters, for instance, are situated directly behind a rather high wooden wall that creates the illusion of being a town hall when seen from the road. If one opens the front door of the town hall, one stands right outside my hut. I spend the days and nights lying here, listening to the reports of my foremen. Most of them are just painters. "Little Father Overseer," they say to me, "what shall we do now?" And I tell them.

Of course the roofers are really painters, and so are the glaziers who insert windows with deft brushes. The bricklayers are painters and so are the masons; the only people who work at their true trade here are the stagehands who put up the scaffoldings and lent a hand with our lodgings. But since then no one's seen them do any work. I am told that they are lying around drinking behind the wooden wall that looks like a tavern from the road. One of them supposedly had the idea of throwing a stone through one of the not-so-well-painted windows in the village, the other day, and replacing it with real glass. If this practice spreads, I almost fear for the success of my mission.

April 12, 1784

The meaning of my last sentence in yesterday's annotations can best be illustrated by the fact that more and more fake window fronts have, since then, been replaced by real ones. One of the glaziers, a certain Popov from Nicolaiev, a painter in reality, complained to me today. "Our honest work is being disfigured," he cried. "One hardly has time to lay down one's brush before people replace our paintings with real windows."

Sometimes I can't help feeling that we are in reality building two villages: a false one and a real one, without actually wanting to build the real one, as though it were growing by itself out of the false one, as if by necessity.

April 13, 1784

A nightmare shocked me from my nap after lunch today. I dreamed that the carriage was finally passing through the village, but that the Empress was fast asleep and even the prince did not dare rouse her. I tell myself she might also happen to be in the arms of her lover, that very same Prince Potemkin, just as the carriage races through our street. Perhaps she'll look out for the flick of an eyelid. I'm aware that all of us are here for nothing but the possibility of this one blink. I have asked Pravdin to subject the gables particularly to another critical examination, in view of her possible glance.

Petrov just came to me, all out of breath, and told me confidentially that real smoke was rising from a chimney he had just finished painting. Since I have no time to check up on the matter myself, I sent him back and asked him to take a look at the various housefronts from the rear. Someone has extended the front toward the back and made a house of it, he called to me from the door of my hut. By all the saints! I wouldn't be surprised if church bells rang for mass tomorrow morning.

April 17, 1784

The dream I mentioned earlier seems to be undergoing curious transformations, especially when one compares it to the anxiety fantasies I had when I first learned of my mission. At the time I thought, "What if Catherine expressed the wish to dismount? What if she were to be led behind empty façades rather than into a cozy room?"

Lieutenant Chuchotatsky called on me yesterday, or the day before, just as I was lying down for a nap; he's being transferred from Odessa to one of the new garrisons on Crimea. "Where do you intend to build the make-believe village, Little Father?" he asked me. Although I know that he's fond of joking, I'd almost jumped to my feet and rushed outside. For days now I've been plagued by a fantasy of the prince asking me the same question. The church bells did ring this morning and Petrov tells me that smoke is now rising from every chimney and that one can see one's reflection in countless windows behind which one can see real flowers standing in real vases. Supposedly the locksmiths, glaziers, roofers, bricklayers, *et al.*, no longer have paint stains on their overalls, and very close to my lodgings, wall to wall so to speak, I can hear men at work. I wouldn't be surprised if I discovered one of these days that my hut is a room in the town hall.

April 19, 1784

I can't get the thought out of my mind, especially since I hear sounds above my hut, as if people were running about. The temptation to get up and look into the matter is great. There is the danger of the prince's taking this village for a real village. And then he'll ask me where I built the fake one he ordered. He might even suspect me of having sold the material entrusted to me by the government. At any rate, I've hurriedly issued instructions to give the housefronts along the village road the outright dilettantish look of stage settings. While I write this, the glaziers and the roofers, the masons and the locksmiths are as busy as ants, painting over their handiwork.

April 21, 1784

I am particularly interested in the successful conclusion of this task since yesterday I was informed of my unanimous election to the position of town elder. My appointment is not far off, since the town hall is practically finished. Within the hour, a second door will be broken into my hut which, were I to get up, would lead me into the corridor of the town hall and into a suite of pleasant rooms that have supposedly been installed there for me.

I am forced to interrupt these notes. The approach of the imperial carriage has just been announced.

April 29, 1784

Breaking through the wall caused a most dreadful noise. I was obliged to get up and retreat to the opposite corner of the room. The sound still rings in my ears. I am told that it often takes weeks to get over that kind of experience. Absolute rest and especially sleep, that healer of all ills, are recommended.

The prefect came to make his report to me. The long-awaited carriage bearing the imperial arms has recently passed through. Work on the schoolhouse is progressing.

Annoyance with the
Older Generation

Two WEEKS before his ship's departure, Mr. Wurf arrived in Rotterdam in the company of two lady cousins. Since his trip would alienate him from his accustomed shores for quite some time, he intended to bid Europe a leisurely adieu—a project the two elderly relatives were to help him carry out. They had hurried to Rotterdam to spend a few quietly enjoyable days with their cousin before putting him aboard, but the city kept stirring up swarms of memories from the days of their youth, and Wurf had to assist the ladies in the cumbersome reconstruction of these, whether he liked it or not. They led him up to old friends, gentlemen and ladies in whose faces past loveliness had long since turned to leather. In addition, each day brought new acquaintances, and there was no end to the scenes of introduction; it always came, in Wurf's presence, to laborious but precise recollections of certain ballroom experiences which usually went as far back as the previous century, to the glorious days of the *belle époque*, as they were inevitably called.

Among Wurf's fears was that the company, growing livelier and livelier, would decide to go for a stroll in the royal gardens. It would take a while until all participants were helped off their chairs and standing; then they'd proceed, gaily chattering, leaning on the younger members. Minor accidents were not infrequent, especially when the gentlemen became inflamed and resorted to handkissing: two of them fell in the process and had thenceforth to be pushed in wheelchairs. This depressed no one; on the contrary, these men in their soundless vehicles now rightly considered themselves far more mobile than the others. Occasionally they'd escape even the briskest walkers in the group, brushing past the tulip beds and mocking the others' laggardly pace; exuberant jokes were exchanged.

At last the day of departure came and all agreed to accompany their young friend to the ship. Four hours before the SS *Johann van Oldenbarneveld* was due to leave, Mr. Wurf's guests came marching up the gangplank, followed by the gentlemen in wheelchairs whose number had increased to seven. To give a dignified air to the occasion, a large variety of cocktails had been set up in Wurf's cabin—a sumptuous suite, including a study, a salon, a dining room and a bedroom. Perhaps Mr. Wurf would never have met the widow Saatmantel, a lady of the world, or at least might never have become an intimate friend, if the chiding of his new friends, among which that of a certain Mr. Mitgang, a wealthy bachelor—if the mockeries of this Mr. Mitgang had not driven him from his own cabin. His secretly-nurtured suspicion, this gentleman remarked, measuring Wurf's roomy suite with short steps, his secretly-nurtured suspicion that this boat did not exist had practically—although not literally—come true. This boat, he said, throwing an all-englobing glance about the salon, was obviously a reconverted freighter, as anyone could tell by the rather scanty furnishings of the cabins. "An extremely sharp observation," cried another gentleman. He himself had noticed the lack of a coat rack, besides a number of other things. These words provoked restlessness. They began wandering through the rooms with aimless steps, picking up objects, holding them to the light. "What a deplorable view!" complained a gentleman, poking at a porthole with his crutch. Mrs. Leder, a large lady, proposed to test the comfort of the bed by stretching out on it. Not too bad, she chuckled, but had to be pulled back up with great difficulty, she had sunk in so deeply. Dr. Knick opened the sliding doors of the closet, pushed the hangers to one side and stepped inside; with an evil grin he asked the others to close the door, but in spite of enthusiastic pushing and panting the door would not close. "I don't fit inside!" he cried. "Another shortcoming!" cried Gladis, a businessman. From the bathroom came sounds of violently gushing water. Pink-skinned Miss Aché was taking a shower. "Make yourself beautiful, make yourself even more beautiful," Wurf's cousins had called to their friend when she announced her intention, a towel under one arm. An old senator threw a footstool at Mr. Wurf, just for fun. He missed and it hit a porthole. "It's splintering, regulations notwithstanding," remarked Mitgang; laughter accompanied his statement.

Wurf angrily recalled that he had been exposed to Mitgang's stupid remarks when still on land; after someone had yelled into Mitgang's ear that Wurf was about to undertake a sea voyage, Mitgang had tried to prove his extensive knowledge of navigation in general and of this port in particular with the arrogance characteristic of port city dwellers, all this without admitting that he had never left this port himself, at least not by sea. This probably explained the man's nastiness; for almost the entire duration of a human life he had seen strangers make use of a port to which he, an inhabitant, felt far more entitled. He said he knew the arrival and departure times of every boat using this privileged harbor, not to mention other specific details, and that all incoming captains and even the chief harbor pilot could be counted among his most intimate friends. That was why he was particularly interested, he continued, throwing Mr. Wurf a sniffing glance, to know on what ship he intended to sail. After Wurf's low, precise answer had been painstakingly communicated to him, Mitgang rose and remarked on his way to the door that he had never heard of such a ship—a remark which, while all eyes were now fixed upon Wurf (Mitgang had succeeded in resisting this temptation), could mean only one thing: that his ship did not exist.

Mr. Wurf had left his staterooms behind him and was

turning toward the stairs when he suddenly heard the ship's loudspeaker. It said that Mr. Jones from Philadelphia was expecting the youth group of the young men's association to report in B Lounge on the main deck for prayers and a pep-talk before the boat departed, but only the youth group. Already they came running from all sides, boys in T shirts that often hung out over their rough play shorts. There were girls too, in casual dresses, and the way they were pressing forward made one think of a riot squad. A tall Negro was also among them, wearing a luminous white bathrobe over his gym suit. A pair of giant boxing gloves was slung over his right shoulder, as brittle and monstrous as lobsters. "Padded weapons," murmured Wurf.

He found the widow Saatmantel deep in an armchair at the other end of the bar. The sight of her had a healing effect on Wurf after the undignified, so it seemed to him, goings-on in his cabin. The widow was balancing a bourbon-on-the-rocks on her left knee and came up with a metaphor concerning her whiskey on ice as soon as they had been introduced. If you shake the glass, she said to Mr. Wurf, the cube-shaped icebergs tinkle against the thin crystal walls and are softly bathed in the honey-yellow gulf stream of alcohol. This type of meditation was foreign to Wurf and he proposed a stroll on deck, which prompted his companion to come up with more surprising images and comments about the construction of seafaring craft. They were leaning against the railing, idly watching the last loading operations, when they heard the dull howling of the siren.

"A crossing," said the widow, "as the British call it, is a

suspense between two places, a state of abeyance in which neither the obligations of the port of departure nor those of one's destination are fully valid."

They settled into deck chairs. A steward came and, asked for assistance by Mrs. Saatmantel, arranged the foot rest for the stimulating lady. She had hardly parked her feet side by side on the foot rest, to the accompaniment of exclamations reporting the difficulties of this action, when she remarked that she preferred this port to any other in Europe. Italian ports were particularly unpleasant, although she did not, in any way, wish to diminish their over-all beauty. She was referring not so much to the ports, but to the men in them.

"They're rapacious animals," she remarked, and turning toward her, Wurf thought he noticed a kind of ecstasy on his friend's face; and when Mrs. Saatmantel cast an oblique glance full of silent, plump-faced tenderness on Wurf himself, he was moved.

"Hard to compete with," replied Wurf, and both burst into exuberant, raucous laughter which was disturbed by the sudden appearance of Mitgang, flanked by two other old men and the captain, a dark-uniformed gentleman with protruding eyes, all the more painfully disturbed since the widow Saatmantel was just about to incite Mr. Wurf to renewed witticisms.

"Oho," she cried, "so you are not travelling alone?"—a question which Mitgang undertook to answer before Mr. Wurf had time to open his mouth.

"This young man," he explained, pointing to Wurf, his

voice rising as it always did when he spoke English, "this young man has disappointed all the expectations of his well-meaning friends." His companions nodded.

Wurf had purposely lured him and his friends into his shabbily furnished cabin. The drinks had been poorly prepared and as a result several of the ladies had been obliged to rid themselves of them in public. The same fate had befallen the old senator who had leaned out of the shamefully small porthole and fallen asleep. They had called stewards who had probably been bribed by Wurf—the captain's eyebrows contracted—because they had not only behaved disrespectfully, but had gone so far as to lay hands on the venerable old gentleman because his ghastly pallor, they said, could be seen from the pier. Thereupon he, Mitgang, had appealed to his friends to chastise the stewards. Which—he pointed to obvious damage below his right eye—had not been carried out without resistance. Only later had it been possible temporarily to bed down the afflicted ladies. It was regrettable, he continued, that the said ladies would not be up and well before the ship's departure, which was to take place in five minutes, and for that reason they would be obliged to undertake the crossing in Wurf's cabins.

"We shall of course," Mitgang pointed to himself, describing a chest-high ellipse with a sharp finger, "we shall of course accompany the ladies."

Wurf looked to the widow Saatmantel for help. His girlfriend, chided the captain, with whom he had gone pretty far, as one could not help observing from the bridge, his *petite amie*, had left quite some time ago. And he had ordered Wurf's baggage carried ashore. He recommended rapid departure from the ship, since the gangplanks—the four old men pulled out their watches—would be raised in two minutes. Besides, strict measures were currently being taken against stowaways. Inhospitableness and immoral conduct, even when concealed beneath the mask of flabby, humorless youth, were not well received on the high seas nor in the New World, he said; and now the Pennsylvania riot squad was nodding in the background: Mr. Jones from Philadelphia, the Negro with raised fist, the boys and girls in shorts.

Wurf walked off without turning his head. The ship's sirens were just beginning their stupefying whine when he set foot on the solid earth. To his surprise he found Mrs. Saatmantel there, almost invisible behind piles of luggage.

"In my opinion," said Wurf, "the older generation has abused my hospitality. I'm afraid the gentlemen will have to let themselves be told that."

"This plane," the widow said tenderly, posing her index finger on a row of figures that had been precisely underlined in her notebook, "will take us to Crete in four hours. We'll be there by tomorrow morning."

Mr. P.'s Literary Soirees

WITH HIS FOUR BUTLERS Mr. P. had recently returned from Java, where the walking sticks grow. None of those present will ever forget how he disembarked from the plane in Hamburg, the four domestics grave and tall behind him, their faces perfect masks of discretion. At the airport they had immediately settled into a cab and driven to the Hotel Esplanade. Across the ox-blood-colored mats the five strode up to the head clerk, said "poet" once, and "butler" four times and then entered the elevator that purred them upstairs in two operations.

Wherever Mr. P. went, he provoked astonishment because of the four butlers who never left his side; everyone knows that a poet ordinarily needs only one butler. But Mr. P. was remarkably good at keeping all four occupied. To put it frankly, he had a terrible foible for butlers. Their way of remaining formal while he was casual, of standing stiffly behind him during the *levers* he held, of transmitting literary slogans, all this never ceased to delight him. Together they would hold a kind of literary morning celebration. All four would stand behind his armchair and read the stock market page of the German Book Trade or, when called upon, give interpretations of new poems. They were also remarkable musicians. Occasional evening quartets were always a success. The instruments were carried by four porters, especially hired for that purpose. These people do not appear in this report. We are merely indicating that they exist.

That evening at the Hotel Esplanade, a short story was on the program. Mr. P. had written it years ago. At the time, one of his friends had wanted to acquire it for the feuilleton of a large Paris daily, but nothing had come of that, because Mr. P. felt that it had not yet definitively matured.

Imagine, the story began approximately, imagine a house on fire at the highest point of the town, of what the English would call "uptown." The firehouse happens to be downtown. There followed a description of firemen climbing onto their wagon, riding through the streets, climbing steadily upward toward the fire. A steady uphill ride. Finally they pull up in front of the burning house. The ladders are shoved upward, the hoses writhe upward, throw their water high into the air. At this point, Mr. P. stresses to the four butlers —the porters being absent—that the continued upward movement is of the greatest importance to the impact of the action. Now one notices a man who had scrambled up to the peak of the roof. He waves down at the firemen. They spread a net for him to jump. The man jumps, but he does not fall down toward the firemen, he falls upward, in the direction of the action. It is obvious, the story concludes, the essential, meaningful crescendo of upward movement could not be disturbed by an unnatural downward jump.

One after the other, Mr. P.'s butlers suggest that the story would probably have a still deeper meaning, if it recounted for instance that, since the founding of the town at the foot of the mountain, its streets had drawn spirals around the mountain in uninterrupted ascent and that, with that particular house, the highest point had been reached—like the tip of a corkscrew, so to speak. The striving of the burgers, the butlers went on to say, had come to an end at that point. They were faced with two alternatives: either to expand downward into the plain or else to add more and more stories to the last house. The fire had put an end to their worries and so now they repeat it from time to time, because in this way there is no end to the constant upward motion. Pinpointed at this spot, the community made use of the fire to—if Mr. P. permitted them to use the corkscrew image a second time—to spiral itself up to the highest height again and again, without having to enter into a new, harmful system of comparative measures.

These additions caused Mr. P. to pull exceptionally hard on his pipe. Since he smoked incessantly and his pipes had to be cold, each butler always kept a pipe in readiness for him.

While he smoked one, the three others cooled off and were expertly refilled—a practice every smoker should imitate. Mr. P.'s literary evening ended with his brief announcement that the story would soon appear in its new, more rounded version.

Mr. Strich Resorts
to Extremes

People who met him briefly would report that Mr. Strich drank his tea like a British colonel who has been in the colonies fifteen years: casually, as though there were a jungle outside the window with green phosphor eyes. But this judgment did not do justice to the small, carefully-dressed professor. The cautiously chosen circle of like-minded persons—mostly students—who'd gather about him twice a week, appreciated Mr. Strich mainly for the ring of his crystal-clear definitions. During a discussion of modern literary problems especially he'd distinguish himself by an eloquence that was downright Gallic. It was not surprising that an incidental conversation about poet C. provoked deep thoughts in Mr. Strich. "C.'s reflections," he remarked, "C.'s reflections concerning the need for provocation are particularly deserving of our attention. We are astonished to find that they have not, so far, been the subject of a thesis in philology. Now there's a gap that cries out to be filled."

Encouraged by his friends' enthusiastic agreement, Strich spent the following weeks determining the whereabouts of poet C.'s manuscripts; he discovered that an auction had expatriated them to Greenland. Strich decided to gain insight into the manuscripts on the spot. And while doing so, it did not escape him that the published versions of some of C.'s essays did not altogether correspond to the originals; at one point an "and" had been omitted, elsewhere the word "mild," absolutely appropriate in that particular context, had been replaced by "wild"—a falsification which Strich called malevolent as well as fatal.

With a staff of collaborators Strich bore witness to the errors in an extensive article which he sent to numerous papers. "We must," he said in his foreword, "do justice to a man who set himself the task of communicating deep thought content to us—an achievement that is only too readily misunderstood, since certain persons seem to have sabotaged the faithful transposition of his works into print."

Unfortunately we are obliged to report that all newspapers refused Strich's article. One editor said the essay would make better material for a nighttime broadcast. But here too Strich was bitterly disappointed. C. had nothing more to say to "us contemporaries," one program manager wrote, he might justifiedly be called "dated"—especially for a nighttime broadcast, which was saying a lot.

Mr. Strich Resorts to Extremes

"I suspect," cried Strich at the next meeting, "I suspect that there is method behind all these undignified misapprehensions."

This revelation aroused outrage in the usually quiet circle; there were loud demonstrations. Enflamed by the booing of several students, Strich let himself be carried away to the point of saying that he would force them to broadcast the manuscript, with arms if need be. "All we'd have to do," he said, "is occupy the radio station. But that demands careful preparation." All agreed; the next day duties were assigned; there followed six weeks of pistol practice, with the volumes of poets Strich disliked and of which he had long wanted to rid himself, as targets.

One foggy spring morning five fully occupied cabs stopped at the main entrance to the radio station. Among the armed men who swarmed up the stairs, one could recognize Mr. Strich, a fat pile of books in his arms. After the doorman had been knocked down by a six-foot student of philosophy, two men occupied the station entrance. With an escort Mr. Strich headed straight for the broadcasting studio. A lady calisthenics teacher who was there, saying "forward bend-d-d-d . . . now stretch . . ." was quickly tied to a chair; she submitted smilingly. Meanwhile all persons encountered in the building were herded into a room where they listened at gun point to a lecture on poet C. In the broadcasting studio, Mr. Strich had seated himself in front of the microphone. With full, assured voice he read his foreword and was just about to start his comments on the misinterpretation of C.'s

Mr. Strich Resorts to Extremes

work, when a first shot rang out. Thinking no harm, a traffic policeman had approached the main entrance of the radio station; it cost him his life. The incident did not pass unnoticed in the street; minutes later the riot squad arrived and asked the rebels to surrender. This request was turned down; the perplexed policemen were drowned in a flood of Greek and Latin satire. A police officer with a year of college fired the first shot, the students replied and soon a regular gun battle was in progress.

The fighting outside did not make Mr. Strich falter for an instant; they had counted on that. Calmly he read his essay, without omitting a single footnote. Just as he was about to draw the conclusion of his reflections, he was, however, hit by a bullet. His revolution must be qualified as tragic—especially since not one of his words penetrated the ether. An alert engineer had shut off the cables to the transmitting towers by flipping a switch the minute the conspirators entered the building. Strich's article remained unknown to the world and the illumination of poet C.'s personality must be left to later philological researchers.

Mr. Paronne Tours the Provinces

WHEN MR. PARONNE, president of Totienne, toured the capitals of his extensive provinces, elaborate preparations preceded his arrival in each one. Paronne's deep devotion to music was widely known—a passion he shared with the majority of his followers. Large concerts or evenings of chamber music in his honor had become a regular tradition in the provinces: but, as time went on, there were so many of these performances that Paronne couldn't possibly attend every one of them in person; finally he limited himself to receiving so-called music bulletins at his villa every night, read by the cultural attaché, and sometimes this ritual lasted up to four hours.

Listening to the music itself was not essential, declared Paronne in the course of such evenings. Knowing that it was just then being performed somewhere satisfied him completely; lack of time obliged him to forgo the actual listening process. The elderly minister, an ex-violinist of an alfresco orchestra, would read the first musical event, for instance: "Cavalcante, 8 p.m., Robert Schumann, Fantasy in C Major, op. 17," or "Somoto Grande, 8:30 p.m., G. Fr. Händel, Concerto Grosso, in B Major," after which custom demanded a brief silence while those present abandoned themselves to a soundless and, so to speak, shorthand enjoyment of the respective works. Only when the presidential mace, which a thoughtful artisan had fashioned in the shape of a conductor's baton, had been raised and lowered, could one proceed with the reading of the next musical event—although not before Paronne had given a brief comment on what had just been heard.

"The second phrase was not satisfactory. The trumpets were simply unbearable," he'd say; or: "That was no presto. In fact I don't quite know what punishment that orchestra deserves."

So that his remarks would coincide with the reality of the concerts just then taking place, the conductors of the respective cities were notified shortly before the beginning of the performance by coded telegram; it was a special sign of clemency for Paronne to order a perfect performance—a grace that was reserved to favorites. The remote county seats of the northern provinces were treated with particular harshness, since Paronne had a dislike for all things coming from the north. The northern orchestra leaders would almost always receive orders like "in the third phrase, the piano must strike two false notes," or "the *allegro assai* will not be played today," or "the violinist is to bungle all his cues." After certain musicians had repeatedly failed in this fashion, Paronne ordered them deported, and it is not surprising therefore that the labor camps on the west coast contained a large number of conductors, trumpet soloists, and musicians of all types. Paronne permitted perfect performances only on his birthday, on the birthday of his long-deaf mother, and in his native village, a small place of one-hundred-forty inhabitants. Anyone in the country who wished to hear good music had to travel to this far-off whistle stop which this truly artistic preference endowed with a never-dreamed-of prosperity. Petitions from other provinces, begging for permission to perform perfect music, he'd answer with sardonic laughter.

The country's newspapers devoted much space to daily reports about the concerts in the Paronne household. Editorials pointed out that, for the first time, musical performances throughout the country had been centralized for the enjoyment of every citizen. Paronne's mistake-policy was based on humility—like that of the wise rug weavers of Persia—since his higher act of will both admitted and apportioned beforehand the inherent imperfections of all earthly achievements. All the more reason then to persecute a) the unintentional mistake, the thoughtless, the unauthorized sin, and b) the failure to execute the scheduled, sanctioned mistake.

When Paronne announced a cross-country tour, dictated

by political considerations, all were surprised to learn that, at the same occasion, he intended to inspect in person every orchestra in the country. Since he did not want to sacrifice too much time to this undertaking, and did not even intend to stop over in any particular city, the orchestras were instructed to take up positions at the city limits, on both sides of the street, permitting him to hear the ordered symphonies while driving through. Sometimes hundreds of similar orchestras were stationed along the streets for this purpose. The calculations were based on a steady speed of seven miles per hour; at this speed each orchestra would play five beats and disperse, the melody would continue harmoniously, one orchestra leading to the next, as he drove past, all the way to the coda—as a rule outside the town hall. When one saw no orchestra for some two hundred yards, this distance indicated a pause, and the president's driver took care not to bridge the interval by mischievous speeding. On the other hand, even a slight slowing down would have led to deplorable acoustical distortions.

Experts had predicted that this journey would not be without certain pitfalls. The calculations were sometimes too difficult. But even Paronne's worst enemies had not imagined the catastrophe that awaited the dictator when he mistakenly entered a town from the wrong side. Instead of the scheduled Violin Concerto in E Major by J. S. Bach, he heard a sequence of sounds that smacked vaguely of Hindemith, whose music had, at one time, precipitated the otherwise sturdy Paronne into a hospital for several months. Already the *spirituoso* which he heard backward was having devastating tonal consequences, but when, coming around a long curve, his car met the perverted andante, one saw the dictator crumple into the red leather upholstery and begin shaking convulsively, a trembling cramp that did not leave him until the moment of his death in a northern sanatorium. He was buried in an oversize violin.

Mr. Stumpf Succumbs to a Misapprehension

No PRECISE REPORT is available about fireman Stumpf's first appearance at Favorite Castle. It was probably during one of those endless afternoons-off, in the course of a stroll, that Stumpf came across the beautifully located structure.

Somewhat dazed, we assume, he climbed the wide flight of steps, disappointed to find the main entrance closed. A half-open window permitted a glance inside: with growing wonder he became aware of crystal chandeliers, colored silk tapestries, sumptuous armchairs, pictures in gold frames, all of which, as he immediately said to himself, could easily catch fire.

With increasing worry he walked several times around the building; eventually he met the castle guide, a lady who condescended to conduct him on a tour. She showed him suites of luxurious rooms—astutely designed mirror halls where he found himself multiplied a hundred times, reception halls with windows overlooking magnificent stretches of lawn, fireplaces of Delft tile, inlays and a portrait on which the large face of the margravine was growing darker with every century.

Mr. Stumpf's complimentary remarks put the guide in a good mood and she offered to show him the chapel in which the aging margravine used to castigate herself; in which whole bus-loads of tourists got the shivers. But fireman Stumpf declined. He was suddenly overcome with a desire to sit down in front of one of those fireplaces on a cool fall evening and tell about his adventures in such and such a battle. "At that time," he'd have begun, "at that time we were marching against the Turks . . ." and everyone in the room would have listened. Later, the parson might have dropped in, or there would have been a thunderstorm and he, Stumpf, would have instructed the servants to make sure all the windows were closed. Or he'd have played a game of chess, with the prefect perhaps, closing his eyes to the flirtation going on with one's beloved wife, the Baroness von Stumpf. After all, there was a certain lady in Baden-Baden— a British lady of noble birth—and hadn't there been something more than coincidental about their frequent meetings in Eberbach's meadows on early morning rides?

Yes, now those clear, breakable mornings came back to him, full of sweet presentiment, the air like powder, dew on every bush. Nothing but a nod between them, a brief call, and both would ride off toward a secret destination. Side by side they'd gallop, under them grass, brooks, and whoops over a fence. Occasionally von Stumpf would softly veer away from the common direction, then turn abruptly, bring his mare to a sudden stand, but only to fly after his companion, cutting across her course at a sharp angle. Like two complete strangers they'd ride across the fields, drawing up short, cutting across each other's paths, or racing toward each other, head on as though at a tournament.

During the weeks that followed, fireman Stumpf found it hard to wait eight daily hours for a fire to break out in the small town nearby. His colleagues, who knew him as a sturdy, conscientious man, thought they noticed an air of dreamy distraction about him that hardly became his sixty years. When he sang "I was once a Czardas cavalier . . ." at a firemen's benefit, his usually powerful voice betrayed extraordinary sympathy with the subject of the song. His friends also detected something downright arrogant in Stumpf's conduct. Up to then they had known him as a simple, hearty man who'd enter the firehouse with a loud, determined step and comment noisily on the events of the day; now they couldn't help noticing his mincing, almost ridiculous gait. When he gave a report, he'd frequently jerk his rigid torso this way and that, and skip instead of walking; a joker remarked that Stumpf carried his fireman's axe as though it were an elegant sword dangling down his side.

Since that memorable afternoon he regularly repeated his visits to Favorite. If there were other visitors during the guided tours, and Stumpf never missed a single one, he would acknowledge their presence with a frown. After several months he knew the castle better than the guide herself; it seemed that he took part in the tours only to find his knowledge of the location of various objects confirmed again and again. Crankily he'd note temporary changes in the castle interior. One day he demanded in an angry voice an account of the whereabouts of a vase which, as he was quickly informed, had been sent to Armonk, N.Y., for a brief exhibit. Those were things one could not hear without grief, he replied hotly. One was entitled to find the margravine's bedroom unchanged. And once he pointed, stern-eyed, brows a single line, to a bush that had not yet been trimmed. The gardener stammered an embarrassed excuse.

But these imperfections did not prevent him from coming to Favorite on that last Sunday—a mild, colorful fall day. One saw him walk past the wide-open windows. A peasant whom he had never met before politely lifted his hat to him. Stumpf acknowledged the greeting with a curt gesture of the hand, palm turned inward, and disappeared into the reception hall. Outside, garden chairs were leaning on each other on the white gravel. Chattering groups of tourists were coming up the yellow driveway toward the steps of the main entrance, a travel guide was just about to begin his historico-esthetic elucidations, when Stumpf stepped slowly out on the balcony.

From the very first words that he addressed to the gathered crowd one could conclude that he was the victim of a misapprehension. He admitted, he began, that he had long expected them and that he was happy to see that they were so numerous. Moreover, he was confident that his estate offered room enough for all and that this beautiful day should be put to good use. He would have lanterns—small private moons, he called them jokingly—hung up in the gardens. There would be a band, he went on, and spreading both arms he assured them of his benevolence. After his address he returned to the reception hall, intent on the reception of his guests who silently dispersed outside the main entrance.

The New Is Unknown

IN ONE SENTENCE, the device I am offering might be described as a cube of glass inside which it is snowing. To comparisons with ordinary snow-cubes, which are also on the market in the shape of half-balls housing small fragments of landscape, I oppose two arguments: first the size of my machine—it almost fills a medium-size living room—and second the fact that I myself am sitting in it.

Of course I did not enter it after completion of the device, post factum so to say, through some opening. It does not escape the attentive observer that its seamless planes offer no motivation for the reckless suspicion that it was at any time anything but a large, milky cube inside which a lazy snowfall is taking place. My assistant—to whom I also owe the transmission of these lines—often holds a piece of paper up against one of the exterior walls for me to read that the business magnate who happens to be inspecting the device at that moment has just remarked that it does not look to him like a manufactured thing, but rather like something that has sprung into being spontaneously. How many hands have I seen retracing the outer edges of the cube, searching for a minute seam, a rough spot, a flaw. And I have great satisfaction hearing the tentative taps of the scientists, although in here it is hardly perceptible.

My current dwelling place obviously complicates my selling the invention. Not that I question the persuasive faculties of my assistant who is forced to undertake this task— there he smiles, my faithful Bergmann, waving encouragement to me, his arm strangely fractured by the glass. No . . . but potential buyers often shy away from the purchase because they fear for my life. I give them to understand from in here, with a variety of gestures, that my presence could, on the contrary, facilitate the first application of the device, since I'd be able to correct actually eliminated, though still possible, "bugs" on the spot, and perfect other performances; but to no avail. Nobody has the courage to buy a first model of anything. Moreover, some customers felt disturbed because I cannot tell them what my device is able to do.

They expect that its absolute newness will be explained to them. Actually they think of the new as a not-previously-presented variant of the old, that this device might, for instance, suddenly lift them into the air, together with this house and a couple of others around it, so that they would find themselves floating above the perplexed city like a fata morgana, or that it might turn into an aquarium with gold-fish swimming about or that we, the device and I, might suddenly be doubled, spewing clouds of smoke. One inter-ested party turned a couple of dials, hoping for the appear-ance of a tidal wave, another expected the device to vomit quantities of darning eggs. Neither Bergmann's words nor my gesturing seems to make them realize that the truly new must deceive such expectations, must deny any relation to the known, must remain absolutely isolated and unknown.

The hopeful backers believe that this apparatus is the ulti-mate product of human inventiveness, a super-machine equipped with all the refinements of engineering genius. "Which hole, which tube will emit gold on demand?" they seem to be thinking. As though gold hasn't always existed. "Where is the key which, when turned, will change this contraption into a dredge?" The fact that this device capri-ciously refuses to serve and is, since I consider it successful, not meant to perform any service, does not enlighten them in any way. From this, some people conclude that the device demands service from them and rush home to imitate me. I have the notion that they are on the right road. If everybody were to do that—you too, my dear Bergmann—if you all set to work, the new might become more and more known, more and more realizable. But until then, back to the draw-ing board.

It's Far from Simple
to Build a House

[for Reinhard Paul Becker]

WHERE SHOULD ONE build a tower? Several persons appear, point to a particular spot. They unfold blueprints, retrace lines, toss their heads back, sure of victory. "By Jove," they cry, "if that isn't a tower!" Everybody claps, but how will it look afterwards, after it's built?

And this is only an example. It's no different with houses or whole communities. Let's say the architect arrives. Difficulties don't exist for him. His friends are walking behind him, a whole crowd of friends. His best friend is carrying long, thick rolls that look like stovepipes. Now the architect gets down on one knee. The other knee, the one that is sticking up, becomes a support for his arm. He studies a meadow with a brook, a rock. He narrows his eyes, spreads his fingers like a fan, passes them in front of his face several times. Then he bounces back to his feet and cries, "This is where we'll build the house!" His friends shout "Bravo!" Some put their hands on their hips, tilt their heads to one side and seem to be checking the location once more. The architect notices. He nudges them. "Well?" he cries. "Well?" "Yes!" the hesitant now also shout, but God help us once the house has been built here.

But the real architect doesn't just happen on a certain spot, least of all equipped with blueprints. Without friends, without flatterers he explores the countryside. Abreast of him in a single rank walk the workmen, the carpenters, with their tools, the locksmiths. When a certain spot attracts the architect's attention, he calls, "Halt!" His call echoes down both flanks. But the left and right ends are much further ahead when all come to a halt, because they hear the command later, so much later that, when things have quieted down again, the workmen are standing in an approximate circle. Within this circle lies a plot of land. If there is a forest, or a hill, they cannot see each other and each stays at shouting distance from the next man for reasons of communication. Then each squats down wherever he is standing, digs a hole in the ground and waits for the architect to have an inspiration. When he has one, he calls it out to the men. For instance he'll call, "Work's begun!" and if the command makes the round and returns unchanged to the architect—which can and does happen quite often—then they start building. But sometimes the command changes on the way around—to "Have some fun!" for instance—and the workmen put their arms around each other and start to dance across the stubble fields, across gushing streams, high reeds, across a nearby market square, and disappear over the horizon. Then construction is delayed.

But let's assume that the order makes the round and comes back to the architect unchanged and the men start building, each at the spot at which he is squatting, without paying any attention to the man next to him. With a song on his lips, one jams his spade into the earth. Another is stacking bricks, perhaps prematurely; while across from him, on the opposite side of the circle, pilings are being driven into the earth. One is mixing mortar, another assembling lengths of pipe, still another is tamping the ground flat and breaking off twigs.

Later, when they change places—each moving to the left, taking over the working place of his neighbor to the left, creating a circular, clockwise movement—when it's time to change places, each man gains a more detached view of his neighbor's work. If he likes it, he continues in the same spirit, blending the neighbor's—now his own—achievements with his own—now a neighbor's. But if he dislikes it, he tears everything down and starts afresh, if there is still time for a fresh start before the next change of place. Or he may advance to a place that has just been demolished by his predecessor. Then it may happen that he lacks the appropriate

materials. He turns on his heels and heads for the next town
to fetch them. Sometimes he meets friends there, they stop
in at a tavern. They play a hectic game of cards while the
construction waits. By the time the gentlemen stagger back, a
new change has taken place, they need new material, and
building stagnates. Or a man comes back, but another is now
in his place, this irritates him, they fight, layers of chalk dust
rise, big bricks fly, another interruption.

Now all have made the round once. They are more familiar with the terrain. They have added to it, taken away
from it. But where is the architect? The true architect keeps
away from the building area. Out of disgust? Impatience?
Not at all. He may be lying on a nearby hill, squatting in a
bush, climbing a tree, standing in man-high ferns, alone
without friends. He is standing in a pond, raises the megaphone to his lips, calls instructions to his men. Like: "This
way and no other!" or: "Don't do that, please!" or, more
elaborately: "Gentlemen, I'm lying here in the sweet-smell-
ing clover. My eyes are closed. When I open them, I see
nothing but the sky. Nevertheless I command you:
Nnnnnnnnnnno! No windows please, no windows at all! I
won't tolerate apertures! A house must be coaxed into being
the way a sculptor coaxes a statue to life—by subtraction, not
by adding. One does not add a house to the landscape, one
does not assemble it, one deducts it!"

The workmen find new encouragement in these instructions. Those who had been about to pick up the trowel, put

it aside and reach for the demolition hammer. Or they drop that too, walk over to the architect, and past him, wander off, leaving the ruin behind them.

"That's the spirit!" the architect calls after them. "I'm all in favor of deliberation."

Now a house has been tricked out of the landscape. They stand about the place, every so often somebody lets a couple of bricks drop, they elbow each other, excuse themselves, point out the beauty of the view, express their appreciation of same; all of a sudden a house is standing there. Someone slaps the architect's back, or runs to fetch him from the cave in which he has been resting. He turns, sees the house and cries, "Good Lord! No! Please move the whole thing over to the left!" Tearing down, rebuilding. To work, to work.

Or the architect is standing before a newly finished house. People are moving in. On the second floor curtains are being hung. The architect examines the house, he frowns. "Yes and no," he says, immediately someone reaches for the axe. The roofless residents come out and join the architect.

Again a house is ready. "A water castle," says the architect, "an underwater castle." It takes several summers to change the course of the river; everybody watches the house sinking.

Another incident: after a couple of years the architect arrives in a small village. Immediately all the workmen walk up to the house they built there some time ago. From every story, people are looking out. Some wave, some show signs of fear. "I don't know," says the architect, and asks for a large hammer. Someone calls from a window, "But pictures are already hanging on the walls; ivy is creeping up one side of the house and all that." "That's true," the architect calls back, "ivy is creeping up one side and the geraniums are in bloom." At night he returns. He takes another look at the house. Lights go on in several apartments. People in nightgowns lean out the windows. Some hold children in their arms, to whom they point. Someone throws dishes into the street. Pets escape in long leaps. Down in the street, the architect is making a speech. He puts the megaphone to his lips and yells, "This house is blocking a number of things. Among them star formations." Torches are lit.

"It's far from simple to build a house," says the architect; behind him the horizon is drowning in flames.

Now the workmen are standing at a different spot, holding pickaxes and bricks. They begin all over again. Suddenly the architect leaps to his feet. He is standing on a mound. One can see his silhouette from the construction area. He waves the workmen over. They approach with hesitant steps, carrying pickaxe, spade, shovel and wobbling mortar trough. "Closer," he calls, "come closer!" "Where? Where do you want us?" "Here, right here!" He points to a spot exactly beside his left foot. The workmen start and the architect vanishes. He is standing inside the chimney, the workmen can still hear him call orders. They begin building the house around the chimney, but soon they become confused, they miss the architect, naturally, they grow disheartened, and by and by, as his voice grows feebler, they abandon the job.

The Obstacle Course

Mr. Faber stood at his window, glad to see the day growing light outside. The sky was not cloudless. In the east, a lazy, yellowish sun was preparing to show itself altogether.

Mr. Faber waited for that moment, raising the collar of his dressing gown. Behind him in the room, he heard the wood crackling in his fireplace, the fresh wood he had placed on top of last evening's ashes. He loved the morning, the few hours he spent with an empty stomach before breakfast, before the day claimed its due.

The night had brought colder weather, as one could conclude from the thread of smoke that was rising from the chimney next door. The old snow that had been shrinking a little every noon during the past weeks was frozen this morning into definitive patterns. The man whom Faber had noticed outside his house had thrust both hands deep into the pockets of his fur coat. "What is he waiting for?" Faber asked himself. The man's attitude had something of readiness about it.

Faber stepped back into the still half-dark room. Distractedly he abandoned himself to the spectacle of the fire that was reaching out more vigorously. The white skin of the birch logs became visible behind the flames rising silkily to the flue. Faber began rearranging the wood with the tongs to make it burn more evenly. Not for reasons of economy—one could rightly call him a good manager, a moderate man—did he dispense with the regular service of a houseboy, but because such an occupation within his own quiet house put him in an auspicious mood and supplied him with an inner strength from which to draw his day's work.

Had he seen right? And if he had seen right, then why was it reaching his consciousness only now, as he knelt down once more to feed another log to the fire? Why did his eyes only now acknowledge the image of the man out there in the snow, in front of his house, imitating every single step Faber felt compelled to take on the inside?

Tentatively he turned toward the dining room. The man outside followed in the same direction, removing his hands from his pockets, probably for the purpose of greater mobility. Faber froze in his tracks, the stranger stood motionless. Faber forced himself to take a single giant step, the other merely flexed his knees, as though indicating that these momentary attempts at walking were not the real issue.

The Obstacle Course

Faber ran through the foyer and all the way down to the kitchen, but when he came to an abrupt halt, grabbing a chair to brake himself, the stranger's face was already staring at him from the other side of the window pane. Again his arms were buried elbow-deep in his roomy pockets.

Faber ran through all his rooms at a rapid pace. First he crossed the living room that led to the dining room. Then, without stopping, diagonally through the living room out into the foyer, which had wide windows, and from there to the kitchen. Without stopping he bounded sideways into a pantry that led to a stairway. He climbed the steps in an instant. They brought him up to a stage-type platform that permitted entrance to his workroom that led—after leaping down a few steps—to the corridor that took him back to the living room. The corridor provided a variant as it was completely closed in on all sides and had probably concealed him from his competitor. But coming out of this passageway he found the stranger already waiting under one of the living room windows. He'd catch sight of him only for a split second as the other man threw himself forward like a relay runner to start off again in the same direction; when Faber reached the next room they'd be running neck-and-neck for a second or two. Then the man outside, whose course was not obstructed by furniture or the crevice of a narrow door, would immediately be yards ahead. From one room to the next he could see the stranger always set for another round. Could it be that outside, all around the house, identically clad teammates stood waiting, ready to run, so that each of them had only to cover the length of a room, ready to drive him on and on forever?

Heading once again toward the hidden corridor, Faber stopped abruptly and turned. He ran diagonally through the study, over the pantry steps, down into the kitchen toward the foyer, and from there into the dining room. Only then did he perceive the gentleman outside, but from the back, turning the corner of the house. Now he might miss him for the duration of a round or two, on his flight toward one of the rooms, see only the coattail of the man rushing past. If he fell into a walking step, he'd sometimes see the stranger shoot past several times, on the outside, before moderating his speed to a trot, or stopping altogether.

But if the stranger sprinted away once more, doubling his speed, Faber couldn't help doing the same. Again he'd race and leap through the familiar rooms, around tight corners, up short flights of stairs, over platforms. Arms pressed to his sides, coattails flying higher, the eyes blurrily perceived the same image: the stranger posted here and here and here under a window, always ready to overtake him.

Who had shoved the glass into Faber's hand that he was draining avidly in the secrecy of the corridor? Hadn't there been guests sitting in the living room the last time he shot through it, guests following his course with widening eyes? Shouldn't they be taken care of? Was this an endurance race? How would he be able to do his work?

One might—Faber reflected while running—remove unnecessary furniture, roll up the carpet, put away the vases which his heavy tread caused to tinkle here and there: clear the arena. Draperies in which he became entangled because he calculated a turn badly, or because he had let himself be distracted by looking after his competitor too long, should be taken down, and door sills were obstacles too. And what was the use of chairs? Supposing one also abandoned one's heavy morning coat, one's slippers? And what purpose—Faber kept running—was served by the records and documents that kept piling up in his workroom? Didn't they fly in all directions at his breathless approach?

One could tear down the walls, install a merry-go-round in the empty space, let oneself be spun around to music. Or else an existence under the window sills. An existence not unlike the previous one, except that one would not be able to stand up straight without being seen from outside and challenged anew. Why not lie in front of the fireplace instead of standing or sitting?

What about asking the gentleman in, to decide the race inside the house? Did one have to fear that, while such an invitation was being called from the stoop, the stranger might slip furtively into the house and bolt all the doors: the new master of the house? Had perhaps someone else tricked him out of house and home in just that manner?

Mr. Faber pondered—while flying through the foyer, bounding up the stairs to the second floor, to the attic. Nor was the idea to join the stranger in order to spy with him on other houses to be discarded. Like ghosts the familiar rooms weaved past him. Siphon bottles and glasses tinkled, a curtain flew high in the breeze of his passing. His goal: to run at his own heels.

He didn't notice that it was getting dark, that his path grew harder and harder, that no one was any longer running alongside him outside.

Monopoly

WHO WILL DENY that there exist, in our well-ordered society, certain professions which, essential though they may be, are rewarded with few honors? The office of executioner is considered shameful, and yet anyone gaining access to certain files at the Ministry of Justice would be surprised to discover how many applications for that particular occupation are submitted each year, especially from rural localities. This is a digression; I earn my living by a different means. Nevertheless I, too, sometimes meet with the contempt the public reserves for those who serve it in some grim capacity.

Coming from my neighbor, for instance, such prejudice is painful; he is an educated man. The modest property on which my establishment is located borders his on one side, and we share the fence in both directions since a narrow strip of my land runs behind his grounds. This man, a Dr. Huden, the director of a clinic, avoids me whenever and wherever he can. He does not appreciate my cordial greeting—I raise my dark hat, place it over my heart and bow—and my notes, which are unavoidable between neighbors, concerning problems of gardening, are answered by his secretary in the briefest manner. Once he even tried to secure an injunction in the magistrate's court against my leading processions past his healing institution, because it gave the impression that these processions originated there. I might have replied to this— had I been called upon to do so—that a lively exchange of customers does indeed occur between our two houses, and I need hardly say in which direction. Furthermore, if my neighbor's complaint had been listened to, would not the baker Goldhart, the butcher Schild, and all residents whose windows mirror my grave parades, have a right to complain as well? Are we not, wherever we go, surrounded by images of becoming and perishing? A fool he who is not aware! Huden also felt put upon by the industrious hammering in the workshops behind the offices—I manufacture on the premises. To this I might reply that the singing which the grateful patients are compelled to offer in the doctor's praise every evening doesn't benefit me greatly either. They gather under Huden's window, on crutches, some even in moveable beds, and offer songs of gratitude to this friend of humanity. You may question my ledger as to whether this practice builds their faith, or furthers their health.

I can feel it, the reader will hesitate to allow me the expression of sympathy discernible in the last sentence. True, I may have strayed from my subject, or rather have given undue space to the description of circumstances that are almost totally forgotten today, but at the time they were annoying and deserve mention precisely because they are part of history. Recently, or more exactly ever since my sole competitor, Mr. Kroog, passed away, I have had, so to speak, a monopoly in this town. With Kroog we also buried the old spirit that gave a bad name to our profession. This old spirit—and I ask forgiveness if I reach once again for the harp—stemmed from the oppressive contact with people known as survivors, an unfortunate, deprecatory name that caused a great deal of harm. Hanging head, sagging shoulders, mild gestures, soft speech: all typified this spirit. How could an emancipated public not recoil in dread from representatives of a profession who'd invariably appear, brittle-handed, at the very spot where another had just reaped his somber harvest? I, at any rate, soon realized the error of post-festum canvassing. I now began to call, not on houses with thickly-draped windows where people crept about on tiptoe, but on red-cheeked, still-united—in many cases, as a matter of fact, not so happily united—families, whom Huden had never gone to see either. There I was permitted to sit erect, with dry eyes and a firm voice, unrolling blueprints and opening brochures. Wood samples were inspected, the grain praised or rejected. I was able to show script samples without blushing. Texts were drafted, the angle of the chisel determined, the plot picked before the reaper had swung his scythe.

Success—if the word is appropriate in this context—did not fail to materialize. I now leave my card with the photographer's at the young mother's bedside. The traveller who passes through our town receives a message from my pen together with a leaflet from the chamber of commerce. If he heeds my message, he'll settle right here, mainly because he is eager for security—what can be surer than the earth?—monthly installments often purchase the plot ahead of time, and he is guaranteed a gardener's care, should relatives later refrain. And last but not least: transferring the inevitable event into the realm of sober planning has taken the sting out of the subject.

I am not saying anything new: public demand soon began to exert a pressure with which I had trouble coping. Strips of lawn were acquired, fenced in, row after row, and equipped with name plates, permitting every resident of the town to dwell out there while still very much alive, and quite a few of them actually do, in the flesh, in full possession of their senses, a practice which makes the final event appear as nothing but the last homecoming to an already previously occupied rectangle. Without any encouragement on my part it became the custom to have one's portrait done lying on the coffin—as soon as the latter was ready—in an animated pose, probably the revival of an ancient peasant custom.

We are no longer able to satisfy each and every request; the available terrain decreases in the same proportion that the overlap of still-unfulfilled contracts increases. But then, caring for and servicing my present customers takes up all my energy. Whenever I walk across the open fields on a day off, the sight of all these people alive and busy on their modest plots relaxes me and puts me in a happy mood. They take not infrequent strolls to their holdings, enjoy the view they will one day no longer be able to see. Often they'll sit with their families, with pets they have taken along, in the center of these meticulously fenced-in areas, having a picnic, holding a piece of meat over the open fire, listening to the hissing drip drip of the fat. They tilt bottles to their mouths and show each other fields and gardens, the village, the forest, and when the sun goes down, they play the guitar and sing sad or gay songs. As far as the eye can reach, one sees them taking care of the ground of which they are sure, the good earth. "I can see the mountain," the father cries. "And I the river," cries the mother, and quickly she sets the table while they praise the beauty of the place and its security.

Of course a fight occasionally breaks out, for instance a person arrives at his plot to find on the plot right next to it a much-disliked neighbor who is singing or playing an instrument, who begins to taunt him, or make disrespectful gestures. Then it may come to blows. Name stakes fly across the fences, one party wins allies, and if the annoying occupant is completely surrounded by enemy plots, he flees, although most unwillingly. Quick intervention is recommended. I appear as the arbiter, under the eyes of the whole town, because it is true, the town itself is becoming more and more deserted. Once a person has acquired a plot and planted his stake in the ground: he abandons his previous occupations, installs himself as well as he can, shivering slightly under a rough tarpaulin, buried under great snowdrifts in the winter, while the fireplace in his house is falling apart.

The town itself, in which Huden is still active with his praise-singing patients, is dying out, becoming what we leave behind—an ever colder, crumbling illusion of our past. Those who, from one of the particularly favored plots on the hill, where I too reside, see one tower after another collapsing down there, are watching the town turn to dust. They count themselves lucky. The town is disintegrating. Good for the man who forearmed himself, who is already installed on his plot, with a view of fields and woods, the rain in his ears, a wreath on his shoulder.

A Failure at
Territorial Conquest

It CAME as a surprise when Mr. Nehrkorn—whose doctoral paper on certain decadent phenomena in the inner functions of logarithmic tables had, long ago, when it had been written, shocked the faculty—finally received an appointment to professorship. Of course the call came from a great distance, out of earshot of the academic world, so to speak, but did not the very difficulty of hearing this call invite all the more the conclusion that Nehrkorn's work was now appreciated far away, even while it was still being rejected in his immediate environment?

Within Nehrkorn's ramified family circle the news of his honorable appointment produced the effect of a match held to a keg of powder. When Nehrkorn told a few close relatives, he had no idea how little the expanded circle of his family was favored by fortune. Moreover, his relatives—and especially those from the country—were endowed with a strong sense of family, and nothing could stop them from arriving at Nehrkorn's house in large numbers. It could not be overlooked that the majority of these relatives, who had shown little interest in Nehrkorn in his previous frugal life of scholarship, bore strange-sounding names. Often, before being let in, they had to push the family pedigree under the door of the apartment; they had brought it along as conclusive evidence of their blood relationship to Professor Nehrkorn, as they called him, half brazenly, half menacingly. Committees appeared from remote provinces, in never-before-seen regional costumes, and left hard sausages and homemade bread for Nehrkorn. Awkwardly they sat on the cushions, holding idiot children on their laps, talking about stations where they had been obliged to change, about the underprivileged lot of travellers who carried large bundles, and refused Nehrkorn's thanks for their gifts in many dialects.

It was particularly difficult to persuade the more distant relatives to return to their homes. Their concern for the professor's well-being stood in the way of departure, they objected. There were still so many things to be settled before Nehrkorn could set off for his new place of duty. Although the call had crossed the ocean all the way to his ear, another letter the next day announced that the appointment still had to be confirmed by the senate. The university also awaited the professor's suggestion as to the amount of his salary. The relatives, from whom the contents of this letter could not be withheld, consoled the professor. He must not let himself be intimidated. They'd take care of this question of salary, they cried, snatching the letter from Nehrkorn's hand. He was, they said, known as a man of high intellect, but as for the practical side of life—they tapped the letter—they knew better how to deal with that. And all agreed to relieve Nehrkorn of this correspondence, which required astuteness and a firm hand.

Nehrkorn was touched by the activity that was unfolding all around him. Some of the relatives worked at the physical preparations for the crossing, another dedicated himself entirely to the correspondence with the distant university, while Nehrkorn himself was charged with writing to absent, bedridden or otherwise unavoidably detained family members. It was only natural—in view of the constantly increasing cost of this family staff of co-workers—that they proceeded to sell Nehrkorn's library. This measure seemed all the more reasonable, since the formalities for the professor's emigration began to drag. From occasional hints from one or the other of the relatives Nehrkorn learned that he might not be able to leave for another year. The provincial relatives, who were present during this revelation, proposed buying land with the money from the books. It was just then sowing time, they cried, and if one planted well, one could still harvest before the professor left his native soil. The proposal pleased everyone and no later than the next day a nice piece of land was purchased outside the gates of the town.

Nehrkorn spent the winter months in the busy circle of his

family. The peasants, who were in the majority, sat about idly while representatives of the trades and professions were, on the contrary, fully occupied. Shouts of triumph emanated from the kitchen or the cellar when the carpenter, for instance, succeeded in making a brand-new travelling trunk. Such accomplishments were occasions for celebration, and sometimes Nehrkorn asked himself if for instance the trunk —that was willfully demolished in the course of such a party—if this trunk justified as much extravagant celebrating, which paralyzed the working capacities of the respective professions for days.

But usually the evenings were peaceful and filled with sociability. Quarrelling did not run in the family; only Cousin Julius, a peasant from Swabia, repeatedly alluded to the professor's idleness. If you happened to think of it, he said on one occasion, the apartment was a model of the ideal collective. Everyone was active in facilitating the professor's crossing, one trade helping the other, only Professor Nehrkorn himself remained idle. Nehrkorn, who loathed squabbles among kin, suffered from these insinuations. To help the helpful family circle he thought of looking for a temporary job. But it didn't come to that, because Julius was just reading the last letter from the university to the assembled relatives. He was not surprised, Julius said, that the university was cancelling the appointment. The months-long silence of the gentlemen on the other side of the ocean had seemed odd.

The letter said that the university was unfortunately unable to fulfill the conditions on which Nehrkorn based his acceptance of the appointment. Never, said the letter, had a future professor asked for such an outrageous salary, not even when burdened by a large family. Nor could they agree to plowing the beautiful lawns of the university back into fields. They pointed out that the particular lawn on which Nehrkorn had cast his disapproving eye had been carefully maintained as such for centuries. Not only was the university unwilling to sacrifice this traditional landscape to Nehrkorn's relatives, who were apparently bucolically inclined, but surprised that the good doctor was not aware that every foot of land had long become subject to ownership in the new world as well. A professorial appointment in the new world was in no way synonymous with territorial conquest. But since Professor Nehrkorn's acceptance of his appointment—written, incidentally, in a surprisingly uneducated style—was dependent on the land requirements of his relatives, the university felt obliged to withdraw its original offer.

The next day brought the departure of the relatives. Crankily and with threats on their lips they left Nehrkorn's house. Nehrkorn, they cried, had intentionally concealed the limited scope of his appointment from them in order to dupe them. When colleagues and neighbors, who often saw him wander across a fallow field outside the city gates, picking up the crumbly earth and examining it, questioned him, Nehrkorn usually replied that it was for scientific reasons that he had decided to decline that distant appointment. We know that it was for personal reasons.

The Size of the Country

So VAST was the country that anyone walking east from a given point would finally return to that point from the west without having crossed the frontiers of other countries. Somewhere the sun was always rising, new areas were being won, or frontier regions were being graciously abandoned to envious neighbors. One didn't hear much of such transactions; it was difficult enough to imagine what a neighbor was.

The number and names of the cities were not exactly known and it was impossible to determine the number of inhabitants. Just keeping up the index of cities, which they filed in innumerable, daily increasing rows of folders, was trouble enough. If one reached for the index of localities in the province of Glarus—which had, incidentally, been devastated by war, since the opposing sides had forgotten that they belonged to the same country—if one took a look at the printed, still-wet scroll of localities, one had to realize that the data contained therein had long since been outmoded by reality. Because the distances were so great, certain localities might, in the meantime, have expanded into the countryside while other thriving towns might, since the time of the printing, have fallen into ruin. It was therefore the custom to ask the acting minister to look at the index books that were piling up in scattered storage buildings, warehouse courtyards and even in trucks, and to hazard a guess as to the number of towns noted therein. No one doubted his intuition—he'd press his eyes shut, weave from side to side, jam his right fist into the palm of his left hand and come up with a figure— and although, as already stated, no one doubted his intuitive powers or his tact, admittedly even his closest estimate was far short of the actual amount.

This was, moreover, complicated by the fact that the localities liked to change their names, probably because they wished to appear more than once in the register. Whether they feared being forgotten in the capital and suffering the fate of Glarus—an unfounded fear, because, since then, the town lists were thoroughly questioned before each campaign and extracts issued to the staffs in the field—or whether they grew tired of their old names which were never exclusively theirs anyhow, because the country was too large, and they liked to advance, in that way, to the position of another locality whose name had just become free in the process of renaming, they had soon dangerously depleted the supply of place names.

Much trouble awaited the traveller who set out for Bischleben. There were thousands of them in the registers. Moreover, one had to remember that most of these were only temporaries, on their way toward new names, just as others were on their way toward newly discarded names, until finally, in accordance with the law of the circle, all would again come to a standstill.

Since the available records were incomplete it was not surprising that the government ordered a careful census of all communities of the country. Every locality, stipulated the government, tired of the costly changing and swapping, was from that day forward to pledge itself faithfully to its current name. Renaming, though drawing new attention to the existence of these places, also made them to the same degree unfindable. The report of a tax collector who had found himself stranded, incognito, in the council meeting of a remote village, certainly offered food for thought. During a brief address, the mayor had called the village by three different names.

Still, before the census takers—whose number was legion—departed from the capital, it became apparent that the deadline which had been set for name changes had been ill chosen, because it had halted the renaming process exactly halfway. Thus there were twice as many towns called Bischleben—since one half of the cities had still had time to assume that glittering appellation, while others had no longer

been allowed to shed it. On the other hand, several names—
and not the ugliest—had disappeared. Census takers travelling through the country were not always well received.
People tried to dupe them, directing them more than once,
from different sides, into the same locality in which busy
citizens had, in the meantime, changed all the inscriptions.
Or else one tried to mislead them with the assurance that a
certain city had already been counted. "Census taker Micko
was here only yesterday," they'd tell them. "An able census
taker, this Micko, not bad at elbow bending either. He arrived, stood outside the town hall, called a number, entered it
in a ledger. After that we served him fresh lamb, artichokes,
black olives and wine. You should have seen him dig in!"

Or else, large groups of census takers might find themselves in the market place of the same locality. Their fight
about who was rightfully entitled to count the place lasted a
long time. In a town named Fladern twelve gentlemen spent
a whole winter. Arguments, which they had in public, much
to the amusement of the natives, brought them closer together. As friends they decided to settle there, build houses
for themselves and work the fertile soil. The census taker
Dankhoff was invited to a hunt at the end of his faithfully
executed task; he couldn't bring himself to let go of the
bugle ever again, and settled down as a gamekeeper. But
most census takers had a deep sense of duty and discipline.
Their journey was arduous. They crossed plains and climbed
mountains. They rode through deep valleys and squeezed
through rocky passes. Ferrymen paddled them across rivers.

They walked with the pilgrim, visited the shepherd on his mountain plateau, lay by the robber's fire. Barges carried them down stream, they slept in hermits' caves, they chatted under fishermen's nets. Rarely did they let themselves be duped by a native trying to lead them past villages that preferred to remain unknown. Seldom did they succumb to the seductions of taverns and baths, and staunchly they withstood torture, long jail terms and the worst adversities of the roads. Even when records were snatched from their hands at the end of their rounds, they did not despair, but set off anew.

Could anything be accomplished in the face of such difficulties? A glance at the jammed highroads leading back to the capital showed that it would not have been wise to double the number of census takers by giving each a sturdy companion. Even before many census takers had set out, others were already streaming back to the capital; it looked like a population migration; several had founded families en route and were returning with wife and child. Delays were inevitable. Many perished, but not before whispering their findings into ears of witnesses. They were buried in hastily set-up cemeteries, which the stream of the returning passed in silence. No one could foretell when all could be heard at the ministry. They were met miles outside the capital and urged to establish themselves in temporary settlements while waiting to be called. Idle at last they began to squabble about who had counted the most localities, each claiming he had recorded more than any other. And finally there was a dispute as to whether the census takers' settlements were also to be counted, and no one knew how many times they counted themselves.

Older and older census takers appeared at the ministry as the years went by, and adolescents too, persons who, as a group, suffered from foot ailments. Whole new generations appeared. Experts realized that the entire system was faulty. No one had thought to count the census takers before they set out. Therefore who knew if all those who had set out at such a brisk pace had returned? And who should have, who could have counted the census takers? It would have meant calling back all those already processed who had dispersed to all corners of the country. Sometimes the widow of a census taker would report to an official at the ministry in a completely unknown tongue. One day, a giant, the like of which had never before been seen, entered the census office, lifted the reception clerk who offered to help him high above his head with blood-curdling laughter and hurled the jiggling man at his own desk, damaging him greatly because it was very difficult to extract him from the formerly impressive piece of furniture. Then there were mutes and amnesiacs ("No, not five thousand three hundred and eleven, it was five hundred thousand three hundred and eleven, no wait, there was a seven somewhere . . ."). Or a panting, exhausted census taker would suffer a stroke before anyone was able to note his findings. Invalid census takers filled the hospitals and it could happen that a convalescent—either because he feared his return to the waiting lines outside the

capital, or thinking that he had already made his report—
rose healed from his bed and hurriedly disappeared.

Relatives in the census takers' settlements who had waited
in vain for the head of the family to return, would take his
place in the line leading to the ministry and the same report
would be made by each member of the family and recorded
as many times. It took years before someone discovered that
a mischief-maker had opened a reporting office in his own
house, thus luring quite a respectable number of census takers away from the official registers. A group of harbor-town
census takers, who met at a tavern called "At Joe's" for
dinner and drinks the evening before their joint report, was
shanghaied by the robust recruiter of an importing enterprise
and from then on served aboard the big schooner "Jo Kirch-
ner." Some ate their censuses, others fed them to the gulls.
The work was tough, but who cares if a wad of bills awaits
one the minute the anchor is lowered? The census taker
Christiansen sat in the crow's-nest, with his red pear nose,
sunned himself and hummed with satisfaction. Whose cigars
might the wife be smoking now at home? He couldn't care
less. They lost their old language in foreign ports. They were
lost to the country.

From one census takers' settlement an innocent group was
led away from the capital, which it never even passed, by a
malevolent group, straight into the desert where the vultures
sat waiting. At home, the rush toward the capital became
unrulier. Large columns of marchers got entangled in the
suburbs. For years mobs stood at street crossings and ad-

vanced only by half steps. This sight discouraged census takers still about to leave; morale slackened. Someone had the wicked inspiration of counting his statistics out with a stick on the back of the recording officer. Occasionally a census taker tattooed his findings into an official's skin. In this fashion, a section head named Schube began to resemble a page from an algebra book. The minister himself was pulled naked from his bed one morning and for every locality in the unfortunate province of Glarus a small pennant was planted into his quivering flesh. It clad him anew. He smiled a conciliatory smile, saying only that his gown was slightly painful when lying down to sleep. People in the streets laughed at his joke, but the cabinet booed at the sight of the multicolored, much beflagged man. And right there, while the mob of census takers rioted under the windows, a resolution was passed, specifying that, in view of the adversities experienced, the country would for the time being abstain from counting the towns, and from counting the census takers, and the census takers' census takers, and the census takers' census takers' census takers; and that the original measure was indefinitely suspended.

Toys

[for Gene Carter]

THE TOY is being unwrapped on Christmas eve. The colored paper crumples to the floor. The son holds up the present—a smooth, blue railway car, "first class?", its metal finish slices the candles on the tree into glittering strips; other hands reach for the toy, while Carl, the butler, feeds the wrapping paper to the flames in the fireplace.

"A distinguished car," he acknowledges admiringly, as the young daughter of the house holds it up to him. "Is that where you're sitting, in there, behind that window?"

"Where am I going?"

"To the Riviera, if you like."

"Let's set up the tracks!"

By now the father is on his knees on the floor. Under Carl's supervision the servants, a cheerful lot, have dragged in the boxes. Shiny sections of track are eagerly pulled out. Tissue paper flies. An old gingerbread man emerges, a petrified cookie, a bishop in a certain pose.

Now section is added to section, the track grows in slow, sometimes also abrupt, curves across the carpet with its strutting blue-green peacocks, its fabulous beasts. It runs in a straight line through yellow and white landscapes, crosses deserts, ends in a furry thicket of square trees. And there are tempting switches that try to branch away from the circle that is beginning to take shape—"Will the train always come back? Mightn't it run through the wall and out into the garden? Across the street? Or, pushing the track in front of it, run to the tree, into the tree, up the tree?"—those dangerous, not altogether reliable, switches that flash knots of red and green string, are set this way and that, demanding a decision. Should they lead off into a new circle? Surge out into the foyer, wind through it and hurry back into the room? Or perhaps a siding near the desk?

Railroad crossings are placed here and there. One beside the dozing doll. A peasant is leaning against the red and white gate, a woman balancing a huge basket. "They're from Bindersleben," cries Carl, the butler, holding a piece of marzipan in one hand, "from my village. They've been to the city. Now they stand there and wave to us."

There are also several stations, country stations mainly, but equipped with the latest-model baggage carts, station master, drinking fountains, even newspaper vendors; they climbed onto the wrong train in Paris with their bundles and papers and now they are stranded here. Crossing gates rise directly beside the track, leading into no man's land. Track signals warn, reassure. The long diesel locomotive stands purring. But now mountains are still needed. The children ask for them. The butler Carl himself slips under the carpet, completely disappears under it. He is breathing heavily, the line quakes, a semaphore rolls down the slopes. But soon Carl's breathing calms down, the tracks lead over a giant mountain which the train—a long-distance express to Barcelona— climbs pantingly. A square of nut chocolate right in the middle of the tracks is removed instantly.

The Mediterranean route should be studded with tunnels. The son calls that observation across to his sister who is holding a dripping candy apple away from her mouth; she agrees; other servants step up, take positions beside the tracks, their toes turned toward the rails; they raise their arms, bend forward, touch the ground on the other side of the track with open palms. Others, delighted, acrobatic, stand with their heels to the roadbed, arch their backs until their fingertips touch the ground beyond the tracks; they float as bridges above the night-dark countryside.

The train is thundering toward Nice or somewhere, for the twelfth time the peasant waves from the other side of the crossing gates, newspapers are hawked, the steep mountain is conquered, Yakuts sound the alarm, on the mountain plateau stands the nutcracker, a hideous totem pole. The long cars mirror one another on the curves. Brother and sister are sitting in the blue one. It gets dark inside during the race

Toys

through the tunnel, an emergency light goes on, the conductor stands waiting in the vestibule, sees the tree, the candles in the sky, the silver moons. Later they come to the graceful bridge suspended above them, on the left wax puddles, walnut mountains.

"Dinner is served!" calls Hertha, the maid; the mother too appears in the door. "Carp," she adds, "hurry up now!"

The father was first to notice that the mountain had begun to quake. Shepherd and sheep tumble toward the tracks. "An earthquake!" he cries. With a tinkle, the signal light drops to red, the train pulls to a stop at the foot of the mountain. Engineer units are notified; they swarm out. The meal is getting cold, but the engineers have not yet checked in. Now they demand materials by wireless, tents, food supplies. Slowly the train backs up. The passengers in the blue car yawn, bite into nougat, complain to the conductor, who shrugs. Speeches are made in the dining car—with champagne; corks graze the bridges. Later, the relay team arrives. Emergency camps are erected on the shifty mountain terrain. "Really! Please!" the mother calls. The sauce has curdled. Reports of further catastrophes are pouring in. Along the entire line dangerously vibrating tunnels, as well as bridges, have collapsed. The engineers hear it, the engineers joke. The engineers put their ears to the unsafe earth, knock against it, drill into it. "The letter opener, quick!"—at just that instant a tremendous quake.

The engineers run to safety, they run along the railroad crossing behind which the peasant has not stopped waving, past the newspaper vendors: Messrs. the engineers are fleeing to the canteen, which was naturally the first thing they set up, a skimpy-walled wooden shack; there they sit, drink beer right out of the bottle, pinch the hostess; once again the mother calls, but they go on drinking directly from the bottle, crying out, "Say, at home it's Christmas today. Let's get a tree!" The engineers are sweating in T shirts, under mosquito netting, on the volcanic soil in the desert, in the lonely valley, in the mountains, while the locomotive purrs.

Outside their barracks, legendary dinosaur-like beasts lie waiting, Lazzarone the peasant is still at the station in Bindersleben, bug-eyed the carp is drowning in the White Sea, the peacocks jump over square bushes to all eternity, newspaper vendors call in no man's land, marzipan balls roll over the roof of the blue car. Wool peacocks stare into the canteen. The candles have been lit on the tree inside. Toys are being unwrapped. The colored paper with the forest pattern crumples to the floor. The engineers give each other presents. The hostess—who is cooking carp—and the hostess's family are also included. The son of the house holds up his present, a smooth blue long-distance express car, the shiny finish of which slices the candles on the tree into glittering strips; many hands reach for the toy, while one of the servants feeds the paper to the flames of the stove. A touching celebration begins.

Unmasking the King

WE LEARNED THAT, during celebrations of a public nature, which are not infrequent here, a certain gentleman has recently been attracting attention, although his exterior does not, in any way, differ from that of other gentlemen. Supposedly this gentleman keeps smilingly appearing in the immediate entourage of the monarch, Kogvägen II, although no one has yet witnessed any exchange of words between this gentleman and, say, one of the higher court officials, whose physiognomies our observers claim from long experience to be able to recognize.

It is a known fact that even the strictest protocol does not preclude all kinds of mishaps in the course of actual practice. Not only do unauthorized persons try to push closer to Kogvägen II—the very sight of the royal escort, itself elaborately protected against irregularities, is confusing. One asks one-self: Who on earth are all these gentlemen, obese or bony, smiling or grave, without whom our king cannot stroll through town? All the more reason, then, not to notice the presence of the aforementioned gentleman.

The suspicion that this gentleman might be a member of the palace police service must be rejected from the start. His friendly appearance, as well as Kogvägen II's tremendous popularity, excludes such speculation. We, who are more in-telligent than our observers, and who advance these and simi-lar suppositions, propose to unveil the identity of the gentle-man in question by other and secret means. Now we ask what prompts the gentlemen—to whom we owe the reports which make this report possible—to be present in the flesh whenever the much-esteemed Kogvägen II appears? As one can see, we first wish to assure ourselves of what is known. But all we know at this point are our trusted observers.

One of them, a man named Olle, is present in order to supply a seat for Kogvägen II in the case of an emergency, from which a king is, of course, not exempt. This might happen while the monarch is making an official appearance at a train station, for instance, to receive a foreign head of State, or under whatever other circumstances he might find himself in the publicly embarrassing need of immediate courtesy. No wonder then that Olle's eyes are directed ex-clusively toward the possibility of such an emergency, that he looks at the world around him only with this possibility in mind, in expectation of a call. And we could continue in this vein and show how each of our informants has had to train his vision to be directed exclusively at one thing at all times; Han, for instance, who is charged with opening and closing the doors of official vehicles, still stares fixedly in one direction hours after a celebration without incident, even after he has begun making his report to us.

Quite safely we might attribute to the higher and highest officials the same one-directed vision, or will someone try to deny that the finance minister's transparent gesture: hiding his hands rapidly in his pockets, pulling them out, letting them disappear again (he told us this himself, which immediately disposes of the suspicion that we derive our information solely from the menial class), proves total participation in the public event? With this in mind, the collected reports of our trusted informants—the fruit of furtive but significant side-glances—about our friend, the mildly smiling, unknown gentleman, set one thinking. Since our intermediaries permit themselves only a limited number of such side-glances and, when they do, direct them to a general appreciation of the situation rather than toward one incidental gentleman—our friend—we may confidently multiply their reports of his presence by ten. We might further note that, with a few exceptions, they probably never see the king himself.

This being the case, we ask only this seemingly evasive question: who, among those bodily present, each constantly occupied with the professional direction of his glances, who then does see the king? The mayor perhaps, whose new town hall Kogvägen II is inaugurating? Or the captain whose ship is being launched? But he sees only his ship, and of that only a part, aware that the cheering crowd sees him: namely next to the king. Furthermore, we must not forget that, while Kogvägen II and his escort walk through the passage the crowd opens for them, only a few are given the opportunity to walk directly beside the king. These few, who are not entitled to the fixed glance of the servant, have an inward look. This also applies to the ruler himself. Of course Kogvägen II is least able to see himself; least of all to see himself being seen as king, i.e., unless he were to order a man-high mirror carried ahead of him on official occasions, like his grandfather, Kogvägen I, in which the latter was able to see both himself and the crowds, which was considered vain. We reject the possibility that Kogvägen II sees himself, and we reject the possibility that the few persons walking beside the king see him; and we refuse to go into a discussion of the gentlemen of his escort who walk behind him; and whether or not they can see the king.

Now the question arises: but what about the crowd? Doesn't the crowd see Kogvägen II? The answer is no! The crowd does not see the king either. Not because the tall hats of the gendarmes who line the streets block their view, and not because people are standing on tiptoe, lifting relatives onto their shoulders, or climbing up on ladders or chairs. But because—when the moment approaches, when Kogvägen II is about to pass, when music and shouts swell, and they strain with all their might to experience Kogvägen II's passing as consciously as possible—something inside them sud-

denly fails and they are struck blind. In the same way that
the experience of his own extraordinary existence is withheld
from the king, the experience of the king is withheld from
the crowd, because, as the king passes, the crowd fuses with
him. A few persons may run out of the crowd into the wake
of Kogvägen II's train, the royal whereabouts betrayed to
them merely by a banner being carried close to the king, and
they may then try to keep up with the king, who is of course
completely hidden from them, and although they blindly
push other people out of their way, hastily crossing and un-
crossing their arms, flailing out at left and right like swim-
mers in a race, all the while inventing pretexts for a second, a
third, a hundredth parade, keeping up with the king, beside
the king, forward, onward, but always separated from the
king by walls of people, until they trip and finally give up.
Well then, the crowd fuses with the king, represents him.
Only those who are not king enjoy being king as he passes.
Consequently no one ever sees him.

At this point in our reflections we stop and try to recall as
clearly and with as much awareness as possible if we too were
king at one time or another? Even perhaps the very first
king? And whether our turn did not come often in the course
of the general unconsciousness that must necessarily spread
throughout a country in which each man sees himself when
he wishes to see the king? We ask ourselves if the role of
king is not perhaps secretly passed from one man to the next
in this country, because each new wearer of the crown always
wishes to see himself while he lets himself be seen? Or if it is

perhaps impossible to see the king during the passing of the
respective crown-holder, because the crowd is alive with
kings?

Even if this were so—not much speaks against it being
so—we now know who the small, unknown gentleman is,
with his mild smile. He alone has neither the fixed glance of
the menial, nor the inward look of the official. And besides
he is free from the crowd's unconscious devotion. He alone
then sees the bearer of the crown. And why is that? For the
same reason that prompted Kogvägen I to have a mirror
carried ahead of him.

This does not mean that our friend is the authorized
bearer of the crown by right of birth. Only his knowing what
others have forgotten gives him his power. Either he knew
how to halt the passing-on process of the throne at the man
who sits on it today—God knows by what means—thus making it impossible for Kogvägen II ever to catch sight of himself (since it has been forbidden him to pass on his office), in
an attempt to experience himself from the side of the crowd;
or he understood how to stop the accelerated process of royal
succession; or, this in case our reflections are mistaken, we
too are constantly threatened with forgetting; or else the
throne was only once turned over to a surrogate and he is
the real Kogvägen II. But in any case he is distinguished
by the highest gifts to rulership: lacking either the functional
or the unconscious look of the others, he has attained consciousness, constantly renewed recognition of the country's
condition, and of himself whom he has in constant view.

Unmasking the King

These, however, are qualities of which we, too, are now allowed to boast, as this paper proves. But are we allowed to imagine them for our friend, the smiling gentleman? Are we allowed to gamble with the existence of the country and bring about a struggle for power which might confuse all for all time? This paper shows to what extent even the consciousness of the mildly smiling gentleman, the true monarch, is constantly in danger. All this troublesome research was required, and more almost every night is required to maintain it for the mildly smiling, unknown gentleman, or ourselves. God help us, should we one day, or night, be stuck with fatigue and lay down our pen!

A Pause Between Battles

December 1945

How LONG has it been since we saw the birds go wild?
With nodding heads they scooted up the trunks of the trees,
which are all linked together in the upper strata of our world,
high above the poison-green intertwining lianas. Down below
roamed wild boars, bears, giant lizards. The birds were
shrieking. In lumps they fell onto the springy network of
branches. Awkwardly they rose again, with gaping beaks.

What unnerved them was the totally other, totally new
disorder of the battle, with its long interruptions, a battle
consisting of a multitude of isolated skirmishes. We, who
had come from the big cities, the neatly limited landscapes,
were unable to imagine, even before the battle, what grenades could possibly accomplish here, besides altering the

Obstacles / 117

already existing disorder, ripping new chaos out of the old. What disorder can a bomb cause in the jungle? That's why we are fighting here. To block the destruction, we divert it from our country, from the mountains, from the orderly paths and gardens, the fragile houses.

Here, confusion, desolation, the festering of war is nothing but a glamorous interruption in this noisy, endless rotting, this murderous sprouting; the raucously exploding grenades, the rattling machine guns are only the refrain. The birds screech and shriek the verses. Here, the thunderous disorder of the battle is only a pause in a much larger, unconquerable, general disorder. The shooting had hardly died down—no one knew for how long; it was jumping about like marsh lights—before the animals took over; things got so loud around us, our yelling might as well have been silence; when a man next to me opened his mouth, I didn't know whether he was shouting Victory or Death.

January 1946

We might as well have taken our time with the clearing of the island, which was begun immediately after the enemy had been successfully repulsed. But we didn't know then—sliding down the tree trunks, daggers clamped between our teeth, looking for possible straggling resistance in the green grillwork of the jungle—we didn't know then that we'd have to wait a full year for another advance that was not forthcoming. I say a full year although there is still another day to go. We are ready.

A *Pause Between Battles*

January 1947

This is indeed a long pause between battles. So far, the enemy, whom we shoved back into the sea with all his equipment over two years ago, has not returned. When we swore allegiance to our god, the emperor, we did not dream that we would have so little to do. Of course each of us hoped that fate might grant him the opportunity to serve in some crucial engagement at some particularly propitious moment. But such vain, arrogant hopes do not become the earnest warrior. The stern instructors who taught us our profession during the winter of 1943 always insisted that all engagements are crucial, and all moments propitious. Each man shields his emperor and his country wherever he crouches. We too. Here too.

April 1947

The colonel said the same thing at the time of our departure. I can still see him standing on the steps of the small wooden house. He jammed his heavy sword into the ground. He was holding his yellow officer's cap in his hand, one could see his white hair. In brief sentences he explained the importance of the place to us.

February 1948

The enemy is trying to trick us into letting him seize the island. Yesterday an enemy ship sailed very close to shore, not a large ship, but too large to make a landing. We opened fire. But those weaklings did not shoot back. Oh no, they turned hastily toward the open sea. Through the glass I was able to see that they were furiously waving. One of them even waved a white flag. Many were dressed in civilian clothes. What's that supposed to signify? At any rate, the old flag remains firmly planted here.

This incident is just another example of our enemy's deceitful tactics. All in all, the war has changed character. Individual deeds are no longer of particular value. These days wars are fought without enthusiasm. Sobriety is replacing personal initiative, cold seriousness is replacing fervor. That's because the reasons have changed, or rather: that there are reasons now. As though one really could give reasons for human actions. In the old days, when people were more aware of this, wars were waged without reason; that's what made them joyous: collective tournaments in concise landscapes, that lent form to the matter, and decency; there were colors, encounters, trumpets. These games had a beginning and an end. One knew when they were over. Now that there are reasons, which scholars with pointed beards understand best, now they don't stop any more; worse, they never even bother getting started; that's because they never stop. They no longer exist in their own right, they are not limited to a specific arena, they spread like weeds, like poisonous mushrooms.

June 1949

The things the enemy tries to lure the handful of us away from this island are indescribable. Yesterday I followed the

enchanting call of a nightingale. It led me to a remote, particularly impenetrable part of the island where I discovered a
large white paper that had been nailed to a tree. To my
horror I discovered that it was a letter addressed to us from
home, a message from my sister. She writes that father is
getting on in years, and needs me. She herself was well. My
brother-in-law had found a good position and was taking
excellent care of her and the boy to whom she had recently
given birth and who bore my name. She tells us that we
should surrender, that the war has ended. "Give it up!" she
writes. "They forgot to inform you, perhaps they couldn't
reach you. The country fears for you and awaits your return."

The men expressed great bitterness when I read this for-
gery to them. Nobody dared express the thought that the
enemy might have invaded part of the homeland and obliged
my sister to write this terrible message, but it crossed everybody's mind. So this is what the enemy is like! Too cowardly
to attack, too stupid for a clever ruse. The only thing that
worries us is that the messenger who nailed that rag to the
tree was able to come ashore without our knowledge. Or
could it have been one of us?

September 1954

In the course of the past five years we have remitted a
good dozen of our treasonous compatriots—because the enemy uses our own people as bearers for his ridiculous letters—to the waves that lap against the island. We have long
since stopped reading them; we tear them to a thousand

shreds, which we throw after them. We've become pretty good at inventing them ourselves, for instance: "The enemy has clasped us to his bosom. He is generously rebuilding our cities, which he himself destroyed; he patches the holes in our clothes, fills the zoos with magnificent new specimens, showers us with coins and fancy sabers, caresses our children, feeds them ginger candy, brightens our gardens with lanterns and silver flutes." Inventing such fantastic letters has become one of our favorite pastimes. We sit together at night and old Yanaga (who is getting along in years), who writes a fine hand, brushes his grey beard to one side and reads his letter.

"Dear brother-in-law," he begins, and already hearty laughter breaks out all around. Even the humming birds chuckle. Others clap their heavy beaks open and shut: they're applauding. "Dearest brother-in-law, you are in error. We await your honorable return. Our former enemies have become our friends and benefactors. They feed us fried and broiled foods, they bow low at our doors. They squat stiffly at our tables and unwrap presents for us. They sprain their faces with smiles and run around with lockjaw. They carry us high on their broad shoulders through the streets of the town, to honor us, as though we and not they had won the war. They consume themselves with love for us. They throw off their rich robes, wrap themselves in sacks and burlap and do penitence. Their wives double over as they trot along the sidewalks so as not to appear taller than ours. They lie on the temple steps and beg to be used as mats. They prepare our baths. They dye their skin. They pour oil over their bodies and offer themselves as torches. They stuff the holes in our dikes first with their pets, then with their children. They give their eyes to the blind, their ears to the deaf, their tongues to the mute. They offer us their pale women."

November 1954

The landing boat was still purring, stuck in the surf at a sharp angle. The mother ship that had launched it was lying off the island like a long, dark cardboard box. The weaklings ran across the beach, which is naked at this spot, then into the nearest thicket for cover.

Trembling with fear they lay in the underbrush below us; we called down to them, "Give up the fight. The war is over!" Even the monkeys shook with laughter. The birds tittered. "War? What's that?" Yanaga yelled, pretending that we were arguing among ourselves. "War? We're here for the fun of it!" Again the birds twittered with mirth. But those unarmed messiahs, those traitors fled, pursued by bullets, laughter and screeching. They were holding their pants, the sad-sacks, leaping into the boat, the milquetoasts, the yellow-livered dogs, clutching their pants. If you hit one, he does a somersault and yells like crazy. The boat is spinning around and around like a mad mosquito. We can still hear it.

November 1954

We made an exception the other day and sent one of those punks who came to us with new letters back to the enemy camp with a collection of our own compositions. He didn't have time to say a word, since we gagged him as soon as we caught him, as we did with all the others. We irritate the enemy, what better proof than the steady stream of traitors he keeps sending us.

November 1959

We're getting older, but the chaps who keep trying to persuade us to surrender without resistance—lately also by leaflets that they drop on us—are always young. There are also women among them now. When we overpower them, they struggle as though possessed, because they come unarmed. If you don't stop up their mouths fast enough, they yell such nonsense it makes you sick. "I'm coming as a friend. The enemies are friends now. The friends are also friends. Make a fresh start. First give up. Then go on living."

All we need now is that they start calling, "Come on out. A new war has started, against completely new enemies. This time we are our own enemies. That way no one gets defeated. Shoot at anyone with slant eyes. Shoot at yourselves."

Enter Manig

for Jürgen Becker

A GENTLEMAN IN FULL REGALIA enters the room. He lifts his
hat and already he has changed considerably. He peels off his
gloves: first he tugs with the still clad right hand at the
fingertips of the left, rapidly, five times, now the same on the
other side. The gloves slap the floor, the gentleman raises his
hands: another movement in a different direction. He takes a
small step forward, quickly slips the coat off his shoulders,
tents it over his head, temporarily pulls it closed in front.
Now a single eye peeks into the room: a spy in the parlor, in
the thicket, at the iron fence, outside, in front of the villa, in
the bushes, in any case once more a different gentleman. He
abandons the coat: this new aspect comes as a shock. The
sun enters the room, and the gentleman makes use of it: he
lights up. The window squares the rays into a bright spot-
light beam. Two-dimensionally the gentleman bounds to the
window, a paper cutout, ready to be folded. Now he could be
quickly caught, pasted on cardboard, framed, hung over the
mantelpiece. But the sun disappears and the gentleman
rounds himself out again in the room, gains depth, he could
be pinched now, once more he is convincing. Now he pulls
out a flute, settles himself, legs crossed, into a corner, sends
forth tunes with dancing fingers, he is an utterly different
gentleman. Manig sits before us.

MANIG IS ASKED to remove the encumbering objects, the choice, then, is his. First he steps up to a lamp, raises the swooping shade, holds it over the bulb in a gesture of adieu, folds it a first time, it crackles. He lifts the brittle form, folds it horizontally with lightning-quick palms, and now vertically with his fingertips, once more horizontally, and the waxy cube flies to the floor. Glaring light fills the room. He shoves the armchair to the door; it springs open; the armchair roars down the corridor, we hear it rumble. He walks over to the wastebasket, begins to roll up the carpet, pushing and kicking the recalcitrant bulk toward the middle of the room with violent movements of arm and leg from all sides at once. There he lets it bounce and overlap itself, catch itself within itself. Rigid ends stand up, obstinate corners rise in vain, are wrestled down. Dust whirls about the scene, outside the defeated carpet collapses. Was that a table? Envelope-size it rolls out of the room. Manig takes a decisive step backwards, doubles over, skips into the fireplace where he stands straight, now visible only to the knees, not much to look at.

"I'M INVITING YOU for this very evening," says Manig. And leaves the house. In the doorway he hesitates. Has he changed his mind? He is back in the room.

"I'm not inviting you after all," he says.

"All right, then don't," says the neighbor. Manig leaves once more, at the door he turns. He looks back into the room. The neighbor is sitting on a chair.

"Now what?" asks the neighbor.

"Let's leave it for tonight."

"Tonight then," says the neighbor. Once more Manig is outside. He walks a few tentative steps around the house. The low window shows him the neighbor, his guest. His guest?

Once more Manig is back in the room.

"Better not," he says. The door bangs shut.

Already Manig is knocking at the window.

"Coming," calls the neighbor.

Quickly he gets up and goes out. In the street stands Manig, shaking his head violently. The neighbor turns, notices his friend's invitingly outstretched hands. He about-faces, walks toward Manig, whose hands sink to his sides, who hurries off, vanishes immediately.

But a second later he is again standing in the light of a distant street lamp, hunching his shoulders, waving the neighbor over to him with a fanning hand.

MR. MANIG walks down the street. It is a narrow street. In passing he examines the shop windows, but the sun slants down at such a steep angle from the other side of the street that Manig does not see the window displays, he sees only the ghostly, sparsely-colored reflections of the street, of passing traffic, people, himself. His image runs bluish across the glass wall, jumps, a shadow, the distance between two shops, now wanders hunched over the arched window of another shop, shrivels to a thread on a brass nameplate.

A man is approaching from the opposite direction. Manig is already able to pinpoint the spot, somewhere on the rapidly decreasing as yet unused stretch between them, which the man will claim with his legs and whole body if he stays on course, and indeed he is heading toward it. Does the other man notice? Manig veers slightly to the left, they scarcely brush against one another. A deviation so slight, can Manig be sure he has not offended the other man, making him think for instance that Manig had wanted to hint that, in his opinion, the other man would never have given way, had not looked like a man who'd ever concede even a small movement, let alone the somewhat tardy improvised sidestep, in which case they would have collided on the furiously decreasing stretch, in which case Manig's glasses would have described a wide arc onto the tracks of the just then approaching streetcar that would have ground them to powder. Thus Manig.

MANIG IS ASKED to go to see the neighbor. Immediately he turns, opens the door, exits and re-enters in the same movement. He has been to see the neighbor.

Now he is asked to carry a helmet into town. Immediately he turns, the shining helmet in his left hand. One-handed he leaves the room, but his receding steps are already approaching steps, one can still see him leave and there he comes hurrying back, enters two-handed, helmetless, a rapid friend. Overconfidently he is asked to go to the seashore. The image of his exit is still on the retina, and already he is back, with a companion in oilcloth as proof. He takes leave of his companion, drawing him close with both arms, kissing him, letting him go, calling after him a promise to return. Turns to the door, pulls it open, rushes out, and back. Again the two say hello and goodbye, tears, reassurances. Again he enters, this time there are twenty of him, many Manigs fill the room with oval faces, wink twenty times, cry "hello" twenty times, twenty pairs of boots, all stamping. At that he is sent up to the roof. "Don't come back now," is called after him. One can hear them thump about up there, slow sure steps, up one side along the gable and down the other, straight across the roof. One rushes out. The company stands in front of the house, staring up to the roof.

STEP IN FRONT of the mirror at night, with closed eyes. Prepare for the sight. Quickly open the eyes.

But how does one get there? One has waited beside the mirror since late afternoon, rehearsing the darkening room in one's mind. Then it takes only an about-face. Or else take up position at a slightly greater distance, along the same wall. Stay closely pressed to the wall, decrease the distance at the proper time, until the smooth wooden mirror frame can be felt against the face. Or focus on the mirror from a wide angle, or from the side, until one sees the frame but not the glass. Or, should the glass be visible, then only as reflected by the opposite wall. Now it takes only a few blind steps. One can't miss the mirror. Or else from the more distant door by which one can enter the room, cleverly measure the required steps with eyes cast down. Memorize exactly how the room curves in the center. Then close your eyes and risk it. Or else look in from the other side of the door, from out in the hall. Memorize the exact height of the door sill, the position of the door knob. Perhaps it would be best to walk carefully backward, to remember the precise number of steps it takes to cross the hall. But then—with head held high through the hall and the perhaps left-open door and into the room. Or else study the curvature of the staircase, remember the front door, start the whole thing from the street, cover the distance from the next square in a beeline. Or else retreat as far as the main square and start from there. Or skip to the gates of the town, cast a long look down over the canyons of the streets. Skipping shrinks the town's image. Instinctively avoid the lake. From here one gets off to a terrific start.

THE GENTLEMAN is standing in the room. Someone puts a hat on the gentleman's head, its wide brim places the gentleman's face in shadow. His shaggy beard is in the dark. A sound comes out of the darkness, the gentleman is saying something. One replies that the gentleman should first please hold the glass. The gentleman is standing in the room with the glass, the partners in the conversation have departed. The gentleman speaks loudly into the empty room. He says among other things: "I am standing here in this room, under a hat, in camouflage. I can't use my hands, because I'm holding the glass. But I can walk forward and backward in any direction." At one point a voice calls: "That's the spirit" from the next room. Then the partners sing in the next room. The gentleman calls something and they come back and say: "No, that's not worth the trouble either. It might come to your having to leave at once, the way you are, just as we had hoped. Incidentally, where is your beard?" The gentleman moves his beard, his partners see it. "We appreciate that," they call. Later they come back into the room. The gentleman is goose-stepping, the glass resting on his hands stretched way out in front of him. They tap him on the shoulder.

THE FOLLOWING may be described as: Manig standing in a park, someone stepping up to him, asking him to step right over into the bushes; just as he is about to comply, someone asks him from the other side to stand at the same time beside the lake, he replies to both sides that he will try to combine their requests, first he walks toward the bushes, halts, turns, then walks to the lake, halts, returns to the bushes, turns, but finally, after several attempts, he stops halfway between both places, stretches, makes himself as thin as he can, even raises both arms straight up, and utters almost without breath that, this way, he won't deprive anyone of air.

MANIG PACES outside the gates of the town. He stands by the roadside and watches the people who are leaving the town. "So you are leaving town," he says to a gentleman who waves and keeps running. Later he changes roadsides and watches the people who are entering the town. "So you are going into town," he calls to a group of gentlemen who are running past him. Then Manig goes to the yellow railroad station. A train arrives from the town; Manig stands on tiptoe and peeks into the windows to count the number of travellers. Later he does the same with a train from the opposite direction. Then Manig stands on the bridge that leads to the country and watches closely. In the evening he reports that the number of people leaving the town every day roughly corresponds to the number of people entering it. "Daily the town is entered and left by roughly the same number of people," he says. "In other words, it stays the same." He adds that the people who were entering the town ran faster than those who were leaving it. Those entering had been surer of themselves; they knew where they were going. Besides, they had also reached their destination.

MR. MANIG is going into town. At first, in the narrower streets, no one can tell where he is going. To city hall, to the post office, to the grocer's? Here one can cross the street and no one pays attention. One can go on walking, and no one will be suspicious. Around a corner, no one cares. Across the square, certainly, why not? Past the monument, by all means; usually people stop in front of it. Onto wider streets that follow the same direction for a long time? Perhaps he lives around here. Although the people who live around here are all at work at this hour. Perhaps he is looking for an apartment? He might be visiting someone who lives around here. Or perhaps he moved in only yesterday? Or he may be looking for property to buy. On foot? Well, perhaps not a large property. Out here, where the fields begin? All right, I give in, I'm a sick resident who has been sent home from work. You are sick and you run around out here, advancing at a steady pace, past the yellow billboards? In this direction? Wait a minute, there's no footpath? Close to the strip of grass? Threatened by traffic, all the way down in the ditch? Won't you admit that you are leaving town?

NIGHTTIME, the gentlemen come over the hill, from horizon to horizon, one close beside the other, hand in hand they climb down the hill, enter the valley. Without anyone noticing, a gentleman in the center of the line stops in the very place he had been walking a second earlier, his friends walk on. The gentleman stands alone, silence spreads, he hears himself breathe, sigh. Other gentlemen fall back, slightly accenting their last step, standing still with straight knees, letting their neighbors pass them, walk on ahead. The gaps that break the line gradually fill up with gentlemen stepping in from the sides; seen from above one has the impression of a vertical line that leaves black dots, markers behind as it advances. An arbitrary pattern covers hill and valley: posts, road signs. Now down into the village, black posts too on the village road, one cannot enter the area.

A GENTLEMAN stands at the door. He is trembling.

We ask him in. He enters; sits down.

"You don't know what I have seen," he says.

"Where did you see it?" we ask.

"Almost everywhere," he says. "Everywhere I went."

"When did you see it?" we ask.

"Almost all the time," he says.

"Even here, outside our house?" we ask.

"Right outside your house," he says.

"Then you don't see it only under certain conditions? At certain hours of the day? It's not limited to seasons?"

"It is in no way limited," he says.

"Do you see it here too, in our house, on that chair?"

"That's what they all ask," he says and trembles. He gets up and leaves.

MANIG GOES to get assistance. Behind him stand three impatient gentlemen, shifting from one foot to the other, looking this way and that, drawing their hands up along their sides, examining their widespread fingers.

"Here's assistance," cries Manig, pointing behind him. The gentlemen behind him also turned around, the entire group is now looking in the same direction.

"Are the gentlemen qualified?" one asks. "What about dancing? Can the gentlemen dance?"

"The gentlemen," Manig replies, "are nearly ready."

"But can they sing?" one asks. "They can move?"

"The gentlemen are willing," says Manig and steps back among the gentlemen who rub their hands, clap, bend their knees, once, twice, stand up straight again, dust off their clothes, triumph.

"It won't quite do," says the commissioner.

YESTERDAY we made the acquaintance of a gentleman who wore a red hat pulled down over his eyes. A belt held his shirt closed, he was dancing. When we saw him again today, he arrived hatless, wore a blue cape and seemed shorter. He walked instead of dancing. Later he even sat down. We asked him about his hat.

"How is your hat? Do you have it still? Where is it?"

"I wear it only to go bathing."

"And what about the shirt, the belt?"

"Almost always without, always without, almost completely abandoned."

"And no more dancing either?"

"Very rarely."

We leave him sitting on his chair, saying what he is saying, hatless, shirtless, beltless, and not dancing.

WE ASK where Manig will enter when he arrives. Just then
he relieves us of the answer, enters, walks up to us, shakes
hands with us while pointing to the door through which he
entered.

"I came in through that door," he cries. "Through which
door am I going to leave?"

We say that we expect him to leave through the same door.
He walks back to it. Pauses briefly in front of it, continues on
to the next, and the next, walks around us, measuring every
nook and cranny, his head swaying at picture height, his knee
at chair height.

"Well?" he calls out once from a corner of the room.

Enters a gentleman.
"It is I," he says.
"Try again," we shout.
Again he enters.
"Here I am," he says.
"Not much better," we shout.
Again he enters the room.
"It's me," he says.
"A poor beginning," we shout.
He enters once more.
"Hello," he calls; and waves.
"Please don't," we say.
He tries again.
"Me again," he calls.
"Almost," we shout.
He enters once more.
"The long awaited," he says.
"Encore!" we shout, but we've hesitated too long, he stays outside, he won't come back, he skips away, we can't see him any more, even if we open the front door and quickly look down the street, to the left, to the right.

WE LOOK for Manig and find him under the table. That's where he sits. We ask him to come out. He asks us for another place to sit. We assure him that there are enough other sitting possibilities, here on this chair for example. He demands that we assign him a definite spot, no examples.

"How is it over there?" he calls over.

"Friendly all around," we call back.

He answers that he can hear us. We answer that he can also believe us. We wave our arms in the air to show him that we have plenty of room.

"No one complains over here," we call.

"One can stay anywhere over here," we call.

"Satisfactory staying possibilities," we call.

"You're hitting right and left," he calls, "I'd rather squat where I am!" He squats.

Enter Manig / 143

❧ ARRIVAL

IT IS NIGHT, the buoys approach, clang, the boat slows down, the land draws nearer on both sides, the boat enters the river mouth, soundlessly it slides up the river, into the land, looms house-high above the landscape, five stories higher than the tree, unheeded in the house, unnoticed on the road, sneaks down the narrowing river, unrecognized, insinuates itself between the paths, the trees, finally a dog barks far off across the land.

MANIG FINDS the street, he reaches the house. The windows are lit, he sees the party. Two gentlemen are standing in bright illumination. One of the gentlemen speaks, then the other speaks, then both speak together, then both stop speaking, then one of the gentlemen laughs, nods, shakes his head, then the other, then both, then one points in one direction, then the other in the same direction, then both point in the opposite direction, then both point at one another, one of the gentlemen takes a step forward, the other a step backward, both step forward, both backward, one shows his hand to the other, the other shows both hands, Manig knows it all, he prefers to go home, so much for the party.

A GENTLEMAN enters the room and all rejoice. His mouth is wide and curved, the nose friendly above it, eyes too, finally hair. We speak to him, he immediately says who he is, talks about this and that, gives information, consoles, instructs. At a certain question he suddenly turns around and we notice that, in the back, he has a short flat nose, a round, tiny mouth, reddish swollen eyes. Here his cheeks puff out, he gets no approval, utters unfriendly words, we walk around him and speak with him rather on his first side, where he pleases. Nevertheless a few persons have stayed at his back, they chuckle and call over to us that there too he pleases, they make our decision difficult, he is talked to on both sides, gaiety all around.

"THAT'S HOW it is," shouts the gentleman.

Immediately the listeners step up to him. The gentleman takes a step back, the listeners follow. They stand very close to him, he lowers his voice, he whispers, they come still closer, they hold their heads to one side, or forward, a hand to one ear they listen attentively. In the rear they are standing on their toes, their torsos swaying above the backs in front of them, their mouths gape, their tongues loll about in the open, their eyes shift from side to side, an observer would realize that they aren't hearing anything, the gentleman is barely whispering now, private information, some turn away, the gentleman raises his voice, the crowd moves back, he speaks more loudly, the crowd leaps, the gentleman follows, the gentleman shouts, the crowd flees, the gentleman roars, rushes after them, his breath on his listeners' necks, as an obbligato.

✤ STEPPING OUT OF THE HOUSE

WE STEP out of the house. What do we see? We see the street. What else? Houses, trees. What specifically? Windows, doors, walls. In front of them people. What are the people doing? Some run in one direction, others in another direction. This causes them to meet. A few cross the street, some cross diagonally, most take the shortest way, almost all of them know where they are going, with or without already or still full or empty bags. The contents of the bags disappear behind windows, doors, walls. And what more? Some people are standing still, some in groups, two are standing back to back. Nobody is sitting, nobody is crawling, it isn't worth the trouble.

Whom do we see over there? Over there stands Manig. Does he see what we see? Most likely, because he is slowly stepping back into the house.

THE OWNER stands in front of the house, he waves, he asks us in, we enter, he takes us through the house. First we enter the foyer. It is light in here. The foyer is in the center of the house. It receives its light from a bright courtyard. The owner, who has been walking ahead of us, turns, points to a line of slippers. We slip into the slippers. Taller we press into the first room. The windows stretch from the ceiling to the floor, we see the empty park. We enter the dark study. In here the furniture is red. Outside the window dragoons are riding by, white on white horses, their lances nodding obliquely. In the corridor that runs along the back of the house we look at flowers. In a corner stands a clavichord. The owner halts, his right arm goes up at an angle, his index finger points to the clavichord, he is looking at us. We answer his look, then follow the direction of his index finger, finally our eyes return to the owner's face, we nod. Similar pointing in front of a picture on the wall. The Sabine hills are painted in the background. Outside, a peasant is carried past. The peasant jiggles, the four men who are carrying him nod in through the window. On the picture in the next room, a multicolored picture, we see a spacious park with few trees but a wide lawn that leads to the bank of a river on which we see a boat. Only now the owner makes a threatening gesture toward the outside. "I'd meet all of them, if I were to go out," he says.

❦ JUMP PLEASE!

Is THE GENERAL going to jump the fence? The field in front of us is already quaking under his steps, there he runs, one hand on the trailing saber, with glittering epaulettes. He pants nearer, his spurs jingle; already we are clapping, the escort behind him is clapping, so are the companions beside him, they have cupped their hands around their mouths like megaphones, they call to him. Let's go, General, jump! Come on now, let's see you jump! Please jump! Generals do jump over fences. Perhaps we ought to hold something out to him? A prize. Very well, a prize! A glittering prize! A prize that can be seen! On the other side of the wire! Idle speculation, already he approaches, jumps the little stream, falls, picks himself up, he has lost his hat, he pauses, looks about him, sees it, picks it up, onward now, in the direction of the fence, panting, with rounded knees, diagonally, hurriedly toward the fence.

WE HAIL Manig on his way, he stops, we raise one arm, let the other hang loosely, put one foot forward, wrinkle up our eyes. "This is how you are," we say. Manig imitates our posture, but almost as quickly he abandons it, yawning we walk on, always north, across railroad tracks, straight north. Now we limp, noisily we drag our left foot, groaning, groping left and right with both hands. "Or like this," we say. Manig does this too, but only for a short distance. We stop once more, open our eyes wide, push out our lower jaw, beat our chests with our fists. "Like this," we say. Manig does it, then goes back to his habitual expression. "That's not the way to catch me," he says.

A GENTLEMAN steps up to Manig. "Do you like this spoon?" he asks. He holds up the spoon. Manig shakes his head. "You really don't?" asks the gentleman. Then he takes Manig by the hand. They come to a tunnel. Both enter the tunnel. It is dark in here, the gentleman stops, draws Manig close, shows him the spoon, asks: "Not in the tunnel either?" "I don't like the spoon in the tunnel either," says Manig after his eyes have become accustomed to the darkness. Now they are both standing on a mountain plateau. Around them the wind. They are standing side by side, four feet aligned. Between them rises the spoon. The gentleman jerks his head to the right, precisely above his shoulder. His eyes travel to the spoon, then back to Manig. "Well?" asks the gentleman. "Not here either," replies Manig. "What if I add a little ball?" asks the gentleman. He shows Manig the ball. They are sitting in a tree. Below them sway the tops of smaller trees, in the distance rocks the ocean. "Not either," says Manig. "Not in any case."

Two GENTLEMEN are standing in the room.
"I'm not sure that I'd like to see you again."
"Same uncertainty here."
Both leave the room.
The next day the gentlemen are again standing in the room.
"Tomorrow—who knows?"
"Not likely."
Both leave the room.
The next day the gentlemen are again standing in the room.
"Unexpected—but without hope for tomorrow."
"Without hope or expectation."
Both leave the room.
The next day the gentlemen are again standing in the room.
"It remains to be seen."
"Nothing to be expected."
Both leave the room.
The next day the gentlemen are again standing in the room.
"I can't be sure about tomorrow."
"Precisely."
Both leave the room.
The next day the gentlemen are again standing in the room.
"Hardly possible."
"Completely open to chance."
Both leave the room.
The next day the gentlemen are again standing in the room.
"We'll see."
"We'll see."
Both leave the room.

Enter Manig / 153

WE ARE WAITING for Manig. A knock at the door. We open. Manig is standing outside. "Welcome," we cry. Manig waves: no. Why won't he come in? Why is he hesitating? We ask him to come in. He looks down the hall. From down there feet are approaching, the slow irregular sound of several feet. A groan, someone trips. "Careful," calls Manig in the direction of the feet. He steps aside. All of us step aside to clear the doorway. Two men appear, carry a boot into the room, set it down, remove their caps, dry their foreheads with kerchiefs, put them away with a flourish, are paid by Manig, bow to the row of us and to Manig as they step backward, slam the door, walk off with heavy steps. "Now I'm here," says Manig.

GUESTS

A KNOCK at the door, Manig gets up, walks to the door, opens it, lets in a gentleman, both stand side by side, Manig turns, closes the door, places himself at the gentleman's side, both come over here at the same pace, Manig assigns him a place, holds the chair for him, the gentleman sits down, "A guest," says Manig, we look at the guest.

Another knock, Manig bounces to his feet, buttons his jacket all the way to the top, walks to the door, opens it, in the doorway stands a gentleman who bounds past Manig, reaches the center of the room in two, three leaps, where he stops while Manig flings the door shut behind him, places himself at his side, briefly calls to him and hurries ahead with short steps, points to a chair, urges him to sit down on it. "A guest," he says, we look at the guest.

A knock, the door flies open, a gentleman dances in, by the time Manig closes the door he has danced several times around us, arm in arm both of them walk around the chair into which the gentleman sinks vibratingly, while Manig says "A guest," we look at the guest.

A knock, Manig gets up, a gentleman is standing in the doorway, the gentleman stands with a stoop, he ducks past Manig, closes the door with Manig, limps over, ahead of the hurrying Manig, finds a chair, lowers himself onto it with widespread legs, muses. "Not a guest," says Manig, we pull our chairs together.

A GENTLEMAN with a headful of bushy hair is sitting at a table.

"This is my favorite place," he calls.

Then he tells about a gentleman who is sitting somewhere else on a horse. Who bends down to him, the horse moves, the gentleman leans his head to one side, and says: "I haven't asked my horse yet."

All of us laugh. Now the gentleman tells a new story: about a gentleman who is telling something somewhere else. After he has finished, a gentleman among his listeners stands up and says: "You already told us that one."

Again we laugh. Now the gentleman pulls at his grey bushy hair and tells about another gentleman, again somewhere else, who, together with a second gentleman, bowed to a third when the third was looking away. When we find out that a fourth gentleman was watching, all of us laugh.

Now we ask the gentleman: "A story about here?"

"Nothing about here," he replies.

"About yourself?" we ask.

"Nothing about me either."

FIRST WE COME to a gentleman. Before we can say anything to him, he has raised his arm, his index finger is pointing in a direction. We start off in this direction, after much walking we come to another gentleman who is hopping from one foot to the other, who claps his hands impatiently, apparently he has been expecting us. We are about to step up to him when he raises one arm, and points in a new direction. Before us lies an empty area. We make a beeline in the new direction, from afar we see another gentleman, who grows taller, finally he is right in front of us, he raises one arm, points in a new direction, that leads us to a side-man whom we had not noticed before, who points behind him, to a hind-man, who turns and points to the right, where the next man stands right beside him, arms stretched horizontally pointing to both sides, we hesitate, until we notice a man beside him who is pointing forward to a gentleman whose back is turned toward us who is pointing upward.

❦ MANIG SITS DOWN

MANIG COMES into the room. He is expected. All the guests rise from their chairs. Some remain standing in front of their chairs, just where they stood up, ready to sit right down again, others have taken up positions beside their chairs, but keep a hand on the chairback, others have walked around their chairs, are standing behind their chairs, turned away from them even, others have walked far away from their chairs, others have grabbed their chairs with both hands and take them along as they walk toward Manig, others have grabbed two or three chairs and carried them off into a corner. As a result there is noise. People say hello to Manig. He winds his way through people and chairs, behind him the company settles back down on the chairs. Where is Manig going to sit? Here, here, a chair is pushed toward him, but it is immediately occupied by a gentleman who looks the other way. Now two chairs are held out to Manig while the host casts menacing glances. Manig looks at the chairs, already they are taken, on one of them sit two gentlemen who are whispering to each other. Now a chair is brought over from a corner. "For no one but you," cries the host. Manig looks at the chair. All are waiting. Manig waves the chair away. He removes his jacket, holds it out toward the company, hides his head in the lining, finds the hole, begins to blow, the jacket bloats itself, puffs up into a grey balloon onto which Manig climbs, which soon floats up to the ceiling. From there Manig waves.

WHEN THE WANDERER wanders, he sings. When he sings, he always sings the same wander song. When he sings the same wander song, I hear it. When I hear it, I open the window, all the way, and go back to sit at the table. When I'm back sitting at the table, the wanderer's head appears in the window frame, singing. When the singing wanderer's head appears in the window frame, which it fills, I ask the wanderer into the room. When I have asked him into the room, he enters immediately. When he has entered, he stops singing, sits down beside me, turns to me and tries to talk me into going with him. When he tries to talk me into going with him, I resist. When I resist, he persuades me. When he has persuaded me, we both stand up, reach for walking sticks, leave the room, slam the front door shut, wander and sing.

CONSEQUENCES (II)

WHEN WE TELL what we see, the others agree or disagree. When the others agree, they have either recognized what we tell, or they believe us. When they recognize it, they have seen it before, or even know it. When they have known it before, we are allies, we get up, walk downstairs together, sometimes behind them, sometimes ahead of them, but always with sure steps, as proof. It doesn't take us long to find the street and the spot where the grey shiny man is stepping through the transom.

VACATING THE SQUARE

PEOPLE ARE STANDING in the square. All is quiet. Finally a gentleman climbs on a ladder, briefly calls the names of friends whom he supposes to be present. Motion occurs, the friends head toward him from various directions, cut a passage for themselves, leave a trail behind them in the crowd. A tight group is standing together, here and there others have started off in other directions, formed new knots, surrounded new callers. Migration, change of groups, exchange, meeting of people running to and fro, overtaking of stumblers, hurrying of dawdlers, trotting of the hesitant, milling of the undecided, alleys, many are sucked in, now in all directions, twisting, outward-pushing, star-shaped dispersion of all participants, a quiet square lies before us, on which Manig has remained, circling, busy.

✿ INTENTION

WE ARE STANDING in the square, watching a gentleman approach from one of the streets. He grows taller, he stretches his arms now sideways, now to the front. As he comes up to us, he cries: "I will." After that he breathes violently, again his arms shoot up, shoot sideways, he throws us a wild look. We wait, nothing happens, we turn and walk away. After a few steps we hear him cry again. "I will," he cries again. We stop, look back, walk back to him, he throws us a wild look. Again we set ourselves in motion. After two steps we hear the gentleman once more. "I will," he cries once more. Immediately we turn around, cautiously we walk back to him. As we come up to him, he stands still. Nothing happens, we leave the square.

STOP! Now move, but not in this direction, in that direction, fast not slowly, straight not hunched, free not groaning, yes in that direction, that's right, a little brisker now, raise the legs perhaps, or is it perhaps that you can't hear me any more, well then, about-face if you please, please another about-face, now back over here, you're running to meet me, that's the idea, I'll jump to the side, you pass me, now you settle down, you wait, evaluate the situation, close your eyes, now a chin-up, now a push-up, now on your feet, now left, now right, now forward, now lift a leg up at an angle, the first leg that comes to your mind, now stand on the other one, spread your arms, okay now a breather, fall backward, lie flat!

WE ARE SITTING in the street, waiting for Mr. Manig to pass. There he comes, already we see him coming. Or is he standing still? We look at the ground, we drum on the table, we are having lunch, now we look back to Mr. Manig. Mr. Manig is moving, but his position has barely changed. We turn around, we examine the house behind us, a friend waves from a window, we start a conversation with him, then we look back to Mr. Manig, hoping to trap him. He is visibly moving, but at the same spot. Is he stuck? We focus on a post toward which the running Manig is heading, we take note of the post behind which he must disappear if he walks. Now we take our time. We look at the roof of the house across the street. It glitters in the sun. There are also windows, some open, some closed. The umbrella beside us, now a fish for supper, it tastes good. Now back to the post. Manig has not yet come to it. He is moving.

"Here, my shirt," says the gentleman, he takes his shirt off, holds it out to Manig, Manig takes it, takes off his shirt, holds it out to the gentleman who puts the shirt on, after which a gentleman steps up to him, offers him his shirt, which Manig accepts, after he has again taken off his shirt and given it to the gentleman, who does not bother to put it on, who holds it out to a gentleman who exchanges it for one which he had exchanged for one which he had exchanged for one, so that one now sees everywhere here in the vast square, on the edges of fountains, near the promenade, inside the bends of stairways, on the benches, beside the shop, gentlemen putting on and taking off shirts that are being offered them, an all-around exchange.

❧ AGREEING

THREE GENTLEMEN are sitting at a table, one sits facing the other two. We see the gentleman who sits alone at one side of the table from the front. He leans forward, listening to one of the other two gentlemen. Although the three gentlemen are sitting close together, the gentleman whose face we see from the front nevertheless cups his right hand around his ear, several times his left hand shoots forth as far as the center of the table in a gesture of confirmation. The gentleman sitting on the speaker's right, whose profile we see every now and then, inspects this hand that is hovering above the table. He looks short, at least sitting at the table he looks short, his eyes are at the level of the glass in front of him, sometimes they move to the speaker, sometimes to the listener sitting alone across the table, sometimes to the latter's hand that points to the speaker. Of the speaker we see only head and shoulders. When the listener's hand shoots forward and points to the speaker we see him hunch his shoulders, weaving back and forth from the hips. The listener also begins to weave, glances briefly at the third gentleman, who nods. Now the listener sighs and leans back, he has withdrawn his hand, now he leans forward again, he wants to hear more. He does hear more, already he is nodding, the speaker weaves, his neighbor nods, the listener leans forward, points to the man across from him, who weaves more strongly, who is swaying back and forth, hunching his shoulders, there is whispering, one hears hissing. Later, when all stand up, we notice that the listener is the most powerful.

A GENTLEMAN sits across from Manig. Between them nothing
moves. Manig looks toward the corner where the gentleman
is sitting. Now the gentleman looks up. They look at each
other. Later the gentleman looks up again. In the meantime
evening falls. Now the gentleman is swimming. Only at
times does he emerge from the water, with wide eyes, swim-
mer's eyes, wet, dripping, grave, then he plunges back under
water. Is Manig a life guard? Should he save him? Does
the gentleman want to be saved? Where is he swimming
to? What is he seeing down there? Gurgling, making bubbles?
Should Manig dive in too? Throw a lifebelt? Come up with
a fish? Manig sets sail.

❧ PREPARATIONS

Music. The public sits in a circle, from a side door the musicians enter the auditorium. Immediately they walk up to their instruments, which have already been brought out. One gentleman steps right up to the piano. In front of the piano he stops, examines the keys. Another gentleman walks up to the bass violin, stops beside it. The violinist takes the violin in hand. Now the pianist seizes the score and distributes sheets among his friends. The latter accept them and examine them. On his way back to his instrument the pianist remembers something, he walks past the piano, so closely he brushes it, toward the wall where he stops. Then the violinist raises the violin, his chin quivers, wrinkles form, a cloth appears, the eye which we see almost closes. The bassist lifts one leg, it disappears in the back, now he stands legs spread, as though he were walking toward us. At the wall the pianist has recovered. He returns to the piano, sits before he sits down, spread-out fingers reaching horizontally, now sticks pointing straight up, now trembling horizontally, all set.

THE ROOM is as high as a house. One enters the room through a white door which fuses with the wall after one has closed it behind one. A corner of the room is furnished: a high sofa, in front of it four chairs in a semicircle. The following seating arrangement: a gentleman on the sofa, a gentleman on a chair. On a white table between them stand: a tea pot, a cream pitcher, a sugar bowl, two cups. The gentlemen are silent. One sits with legs crossed, a hand supporting the chin, he looks straight ahead, the other keeps both feet parallel, one beside the other, he is leaning back, his eyes are cast down. Now both gentlemen lean forward, take the cups, a clinking sound, they drink, they swallow, replace the cups, a clinking sound, they lean back, stretch, again quiet reigns. Now one gets up, the other immediately does the same, both stand facing each other, walk around the table, sit down, they have changed seats, they sit quietly. Later, one turns his head, the other follows the direction of his eyes, both look out the window. Still later they drink more tea.

❧ ENCOUNTER (II)

A GENTLEMAN leaves the house. He steps into the street. The street is empty. The gentleman crosses the street and enters the park. The park is across from the house. The park is empty. Two paths run in different directions. The gentleman hesitates. He examines the lawn between the two paths. On the lawn stands a bird. The gentleman chooses a path. Out of a bush steps a second gentleman, walks up to the first gentleman. The second gentleman is tall. The first gentleman stops. The gentlemen stand facing each other. "You've come out of the house," says the second gentleman and points back to the house from which the first gentleman has come. The first gentleman says: "I did not come out of the house." The second gentleman steps back into the bushes, while the first gentleman continues on his way, a trifle faster.

Isn't that Manig? Elbows pressed to sides trot trot down the street! Head nods in front of shop windows, knees high, straight, clack clack and around the corner. What is he up to? There comes Manig around the corner! Manig trots, eyes straight ahead, set for a long-distance run, for quite some time already, for quite some time still. Are we allowed to follow? Over here, and here, around corners, now straight ahead, at runner's pace. Here we come. What do we see? In front of us we see Manig's back, behind us a long line of followers. See us trot!

❦ OBSERVATION

WHEN WE LOOK through the window into the room, we see a gentleman sitting at a table. In another room, a gentleman is standing beside a cupboard. In the third room we look into, two gentlemen are standing behind a table. In another room a gentleman is pacing. In another room five gentlemen sit, each turned away from the others, all are reading. In another room, already in the next to last house in the village, a gentleman stands and sings. In the last house, two gentlemen sit facing each other. One sings, another is beating time for him. In the last room of the last house a gentleman lies in bed. Who knows whether it is different in the next village. Peace everywhere.

THE FOLLOWING happened on this occasion: a gentleman stood up, knocked against his glass with a spoon, all looked up at him, his face was now high above them, all could observe how he took hold of his chair, turned it around, set it down again, now his back was turned toward the diners. A gentleman jumped up, let his flat, spread-out hands float in front of him, sank slowly, a drowning sleepwalker, until his chin rested on the edge of the table, wedged in between his shoulders, only the eyes still wandering. Only now Manig rose, and stepped up onto the table. Up there he put his feet close together. The other guests remained seated at their places.

❧ SAILORS IN A STORM

WHAT DO SAILORS do in a storm? When they are on land? Three of them? In the street? Besides it is raining, their blue caps glisten, their trousers clap, slap about their legs? Two thin sailors and one fat sailor? Two strong sailors and one weak one? Two young and one old one? Two tall and one short? And far away from the ship? Not even in the proximity of the port? Nothing chugs here, nothing churns or eddies, no megaphone voice? Far away from the masts? The planks don't rear up? And alone in the street? When the short-winded among them starts complaining, when he is almost blown away?

Sailors who are surprised by a rain storm in the street, far from the ship, who see no one else around whom they ought to help, but hear their friend complain and must fear that the next gust will blow him away, take hold of their friend, one grabs him by the arms, the other by the legs, they lift him up and carry him to safety.

How DOES ONE paint Manig? Well, there he sits motionless on the chair. Between painter and Manig a table. From the right, sunshine. Infiltration of the sunshine through a series of closed garden gates that lead into a small front garden that leads onto a small street that leads into a barely larger street that leads into a larger street that leads into a small street that leads back to the street that is bordered by front gardens, behind one of which is a series of garden gates behind which Manig sits with the painter. Now start to paint Manig.

🌷 GAMES (I)

THE GENTLEMEN are standing in the street, each in front of a house. Briefly they nod to one another, and enter the houses. Each closes the door behind him, the cool corridor receives him, he walks the few steps to the foot of the stairs, bounds up the first steps, exuberantly, then slowly climbs the stairs, his hand sliding along the banister. On the landings he halts briefly, his eyes roam through the window across the back gardens, he sees the courtyards, then he climbs on, past the apartment doors, noticing the brass name plates, higher and higher, as far as the attic door, which he unlocks. He enters the attic, ducks around the pillar, under the wash, reaches the attic window, pushes it open high up into the sky, folds it over outside on the roof, squeezes himself through the opening, stands half outside, air surrounds him, he salutes his friends, both sides bow to both sides, and wave too, turning a widespread hand in the air, until the last of them emerges, visible as far as the hips. He protrudes obliquely, claps his hands, immediately the friends disappear, each rushes blindly to the corridor, leaps from landing to landing, rushes down the stairs, flies through the hall, shoots through the front door straight out onto the pavement where he halts, panting. Soon the last one arrives. He hardly has time to halt safely, the others step up to him, point to him, push him back inside his house, lock him in, move on.

A GENTLEMAN demonstrates something, he twists and turns, spreads his arms, is he going to fly? He tiptoes sideways, circles an invisible obstacle, steps forward, nods into the void. The other gentlemen look on, the gentleman turns on one leg, then returns to his starting position on both legs, reaches behind him, seizes the tail of his coat, lifts it, skips, calls: "Is this something? Or isn't it? Perhaps not? Look at me! Now from this side! There! Well, do you like it? From this angle? Sideways, also all right? Any difference?"

The gentlemen imitate, they fall, lie stretched out on their elbows, straighten up, skip, slide, fall, cry: "Whoopee!"

🌱 GAMES (III)

"Something will surely come."
"We're already walking toward something."
We show each other what can be seen on both sides.
"Nothing but solid objects."
We walk through the town.
"There are still lots of things."
"Lots of things are standing."
We continue to walk through the town, our friend is holding the scissors in front of him. Will something come for him to snip, so it will fall to the ground on either side? Flags, letters, coats?
"Then we'll step over it."
"Snip it and step over it."
"Nothing down here," says our friend. He is tired. Someone else takes over the scissors. He lets them snip in the void. They cut their way through the air. Bad down here.

TWO GENTLEMEN stand motionless on a stoop. One gentleman stands to the right of the door, the other gentleman
stands to the left of the door. Neither moves, neither holds
anything in his hands. Now two more gentlemen come running down the middle of the street. They take their time.
They reach the house, turn and walk up to the gentlemen
there. All four examine each other. Then the new gentlemen
step close together and mount the steps to the door, while
the first gentlemen immediately abandon their places and
walk down the steps. They arrive at the foot, immediately
run off into the middle of the street. Meanwhile the new
gentlemen have taken up positions on both sides of the door.
This is repeated.

❦ GAMES (v)

FIRST A GENTLEMAN throws a hard ball, then three further gentlemen, alternating with the first gentleman, throw three balls each, which sometimes touch the first ball, sometimes the other balls, which either push them away from the first ball or roll them closer to it. The last ball is thrown by the first gentleman. He has a mustache. He holds the last ball between index finger and thumb, shows it to us, then he throws it, but where does it land? It does not land, the ball is gone. Where has the ball gone? We look back to the gentleman's hand, which is still raised, empty in the air, no ripples in the pond, no passerby screaming that he's been hit, nothing plops to the ground, no rustling in the tree, no bird cries, the glass is not shattering, the wash hangs quietly, no garden chair rumbles, the lawn reveals no ball, well, where is the ball?

TWO GENTLEMEN make an appointment, but in addition to that each sends a friend to a given place. These friends of the friends also walk up to each other at the proper time at the given place, peel off their gloves, rejoice in meeting. Immediately afterwards they make a new appointment at a different place, immediately walk off in opposite directions, visit friends and send them also to a given place, where these friends greet each other, in turn make an appointment, walk away, find friends whom they send to a place they have thought up. On their separate ways these two will see gentlemen standing here and there throughout the town, shaking hands, making appointments, walking away from each other, soon many gentlemen know each other, the town is humming, a stranger who is driving through it says: "This is a friendly town."

❦ GAMES (VII)

ALL OF US step out into the street, hand in hand we cross, the people who are walking toward us must duck low to slide under our arms, we walk diagonally across the square, traffic is already slowing down, we raise our knees as we walk, first one knee, then the other, we nod, we turn our heads, we surround shoppers, regroup them at this or that end of the line which stretches further and further to the left and to the right, soon they have joined us, we mass in front of houses, we snake across bridges, we surround the river, hand in hand, walking, from both banks, we dance through the streets, at crossings we're already meeting, already we are trailing through all the houses, meeting hand in hand in the kitchens, climbing up stairs and down stairs all at once, we hear that we have conquered the country, now we fold our arms, we come and go everywhere.

MY DEAR FRIEND Manig stands in front of the house, near a bush on the evenly cut lawn. He's probably coming to see me. Should I wave to him? No, it's probably not necessary. Perhaps he hasn't seen me sitting on the porch, dark-green and shadowy, in the wicker chair, white-varnished, glass in hand. Well, dear Manig, come closer. Well, come on up, dear friend. Up the few more steps and we're in each other's arms. Is the bush increasing, is the bush spreading, or is it Manig who is shrinking? Why this hesitation? As always it is cool on the terrace. Manig would be welcome. Does he seriously expect me to get up, push back the chair, open my arms and call to him: Welcome, dear Manig? Could he, before coming, expect that I'd see him first? Maybe I'm mistaken. Manig skips back, bouncing from tiptoe to tiptoe. I look into the glass and I look toward the bush. Bush, garden, chair, glass, house, perhaps we are growing and only Manig remains the same? Or perhaps I am expanding? Does one hear cracking? Manig is moving away, backward. He shrinks into the distance. Now he is the size of a pencil. He has reached the neighbor's fence. The distance makes his retreat seem nimbler and nimbler. No difference between leaping and standing. He has reached the edge of the field. There his figure becomes a black line that touches a glass globe over which he wanders. When he has shrunk to comma size, I finally get up, but sit down again immediately, because he has disappeared altogether.

Enter Manig / *183*